The Year of

Destroying Angels

Rev. James R. Hawk

To our sons...Tim, Todd, Chris

and grandchildren

Sarah, Parker, Brady, Conley, & Ridley

Contents

Introduction

Genealogists and descendants of German immigrants refer to the deaths of thousands while sailing to America in 1738 as the "Year of Destroying Angels." This author's examination of political and social conditions in Rotterdam in 1738 reveals more "down-to-earth" explanations for the tragedies at sea. This finding emerged from an analysis of the 1738 Atlantic crossings, which included the ship *Thistle* carrying Michael Grindstaff, the ancestral grandfather of this author's wife, Darlene (Grindstaff) Hawk. For the next two centuries, Michael and his descendants resided in Johnson County, Tennessee, until the construction of a TVA dam in 1948 forced the removal of the clannish families, including Darlene's grandparents and parents. Her grandfather passed down stories of the crossing.

Prologue: "Burn the Palatinate!"

Michael Grindstaff's family resisted moving to America for years owing to personal stubbornness and the hope for better times in their own country, but the year 1738 represented a watershed year. The French soldiers' unrelenting aggression and oppressive taxation provided little optimism. The Grindstaffs, like others in the Delaware-sized Lower Palatinate, had long accepted the description "pigheaded and stubborn," given them by German Catholic leaders; yet, physical pleasures of Zweibrucken were gone by 1738.

After Martin Luther's complaints against Catholicism in 1517, Protestantism swept over much of Europe by the 1600s. Gutenberg's moveable printing press revolutionized the availability of the Bible, replacing papal dogmas. However, disagreements escalated into open clashes. The Thirty Years War (1618-1648) and the Nine Years War (1688-1697) were two major conflicts that almost destroyed the Lower Palatinate.

The Thirty Years War was a continuation of dissensions sparked by the Reformation, resulting in open conflict between Catholics and Protestants across Europe. The war turned into one of the longest and most deadly conflicts in European history. Battle, starvation, and disease claimed the lives of four to eight million people. Some nations saw significant reductions in population.

The Grindstaff land near the French border was a constant trampling ground for soldiers of King Louis XIII, an ardent Catholic. Towns of the Lower Palatinate were devastated. Wolves roamed farmlands. Hunger abounded. Kuhn stated that some residents ate grass. French, Spanish, Italian, Dutch, and Swedish forces set fire to hundreds of towns and villages across Germany. The Palatinate lost almost 400,000 individuals throughout the protracted conflict. The Treaty of Westphalia in 1648 marked the end of warfare, but the Palatinate remained weak and divided for years.

Other nations had lured France, led by King Louis XIII, into the Thirty Years' War. However, Louis' son, King Louis IV, deliberately launched the incendiary Nine Years War before the Palatinate had fully recovered from the Thirty Years War, by sending 40,000 troops into the Lower Palatinate.

Numerous toll castles along the Rhine benefited the Palatinate at the expense of France, infuriating the flamboyant young Louis, who had long coveted the lush regions around the Neckar and Rhine Rivers.

The Nine Years War in the Palatinate caused significant devastation to Rhine castles, including damage to the city, Heidelberg. In 1689,

fires destroyed Mainz, Worms, Mannheim, and
Speyer. French troops set fire to more than 20
towns and historical sites. For years, King Louis
XIV held lands along the Rhine and levied high
taxes on the Palatines, allegedly to finance his often-
perverse lifestyle at Versailles. The small monarch
popularized red high-heeled shoes, and courtiers
enjoyed watching him undress and bathe. Louis, the
"Sun god,"saw himself as the owner of his people.

When Louis' French war council decided to
impose the decree "Brulez le Patinat!" ("Burn the
Palatinate!"), they were met with resistance from a
foreign alliance. The conflict ended in 1697 with the
Peace of Ryswick, but the devastated countryside
suffered for years.

Wintertime of Despair, Springtime of Hope

The fields are ruined, the ground is dried up; the grain is destroyed, the new wine is dried up, the oil fails. Despair, you farmers, wail, you vine growers; grieve for the wheat and the barley, because the harvest of the field is destroyed. The vine is dried up and the fig tree is withered; the pomegranate, the palm and the apple tree— all the trees of the field are dried up. (Joel 1:10-12, NIV)

By 1738, the border incursions of French soldiers had made a wasteland of the livelihood of the Grindstaff families, with little hope to continue in Zweibrucken. Images of blackened hillsides, smoldering vineyards, ruined fruit trees, and burned villages and farmhouses left twelve-year-old Michael Grindstaff emotionally scarred. Towns in the Lower Palatinate experienced devastation and abandonment. Wolves prowled farmlands. The beloved house in Hornback near the French border was no longer the same.

Hopes faded that religious wars would end, that high taxes would be lowered, and that French border incursions would cease. Long faces admitted to the derogatory old criticisms, such as "pigheaded and stubborn." Outsiders occasionally referred to them as "poor Palatines," a polite designation that could suggest both economic hardship and inferiority. The Grindstaff's, like their impoverished neighbors, knew they had waited too long for living conditions to improve in the Lower Palatinate.

The approaching winter brought emotional strains to the Grindstaffs when confronted with leaving Zweibrucken for America. Summer had ended with only a scant harvest. Resources were limited, and Michael's grandfather Dietrich was unable to travel. Suffering neighbors could offer no resources.

The most troubling fear of emigration for Michael's family was the possibility of family members being separated from an indenture. With Caribbean or British Navy indentures, repayment could take years.

The Grindstaffs contemplated a group-sponsored trip to America rather than setting out alone. The French government had partially sponsored the 1720 emigration project, which brought 4000 emigrants to the Louisiana coast, but only a few hundred survived the fevers at sea.

Was there not a sponsored group with which to make the long journey? Some religious endeavors? Was there a government initiative that aimed to ease the migration? As far back as 1709, the English authorities had led 12,000 immigrants away from the homeland, although 1000s died while on crammed ships

Older Palatines recalled William Penn's invitations to Pennsylvania, touting the religious freedoms, the generous assistance, and the political climate of the territory, which was a debt payment to Penn's late father from King Charles.

In addition to Penn's encouragements, the return of many Palatines from America for home visits served as motivation to emigrate. Their glowing reports of a better life influenced thousands to leave the Palatinate. Shipping firms, ship captains, and business interests in America paid these returnees, often referred to as "Newlanders," to serve as recruiters. The Newlander's business had grown from infancy in earlier years into a steady enterprise by 1737.

However, scam deals occasionally tarnished Newlander reputations. With some immigrants, Newlanders deceived their clients into believing they would require minimal supplies for their voyage, thereby forcing the unsuspecting migrant to pay the ship storekeeper exorbitant prices when their contracted rations ran out at sea. In another deception, some Newlanders misled emigrants by promising room on the ship for furniture and special items, only to later claim the space for themselves, leaving emigrant belongings behind or selling them for minimal money

Resigned to the necessity of individual families traveling alone to America, the Grindstaff families contemplated potential destinations such as Pennsylvania, Georgia, Massachusetts, New York, Virginia, or Carolina.

Immigrants had the choice of many competitive shippers before a departure in 1738—Hope & Co., the Steadman Brothers, John Dick, William and Morris, Charles Smith, and George Parish, to mention a few (Grub). In the Philadelphia market, a diverse group of large, small, and independent shippers participated, but none maintained a significant monopoly. Philadelphia was the choice destination of Palatine immigrants because many who had previously settled there enjoyed religious freedom and unique livelihood opportunities.

Michael's Uncle Barth discovered that some shippers, notably the Hope Brothers, did not require advance payment in cash, signatures, or indentures. This redemptioner system, which started in Rotterdam, favored poor emigrants by allowing them to arrange payment after arrival, perhaps by

borrowing from American relatives or by

contracting to servitude. The Hope Brothers may

have enjoyed a brief monopoly (Grubb).

We Have Not Passed This Way Before

(Joshua 3:4, KJV)

Early in the spring of 1738, Nichol and
Barbara assisted twelve-year-old Johann Michael
Grindstaff (aka Cransdorf) in a scow for a weeks-
long journey down the Rhine River to Rotterdam for
their voyage to Philadelphia. Joining them were
Michael's 19-year-old sister Anna Rosina and
Nichol's brother Johann Bartholomew with his wife.
An ailing father, Dietrich, stayed behind at
Zweibrucken, near the once-favored family home at
Hornbach.

"Gohn of Rimschweiler, Fredrick Cromer of Rimschweiler, Barthel Cransdorf, Nickel Cransdorf, of that place, all six with their wives and children to America— *List of Emigrants from Zweibrucken, September 19, 1738, ship Thistle.*"

The peculiarity of long-term memories enabled Michael to later recall much of the excitement of the journey to Rotterdam and beyond. Shades of darkness permitted an escape from the ruling German Elector's edict against emigration. Michael and his family had never passed this way before.

Weeks on the winding river were filled with ever-changing events: overnight stops, changing of boats and boatsmen, bickering, food wastefulness,

16

frenzied celebrations, fiddle playing and dancing, petty thefts, a terrifying knife fight, freezing rains from a lingering winter, up to thirty time-consuming and costly territorial toll castles along the river (some with chains across the river), towns attempting a travel tax, and congestion from barge traffic.

A particular incident on the river left a memorable impression on everyone onboard—that of the minister, who initially drew attention by standing in the boat and encouraging the passengers to sing some old church songs. The singing went well for a few mornings until the minister started a narrative about an earlier memorable winter.

His story was about the catastrophic freeze during the winter of 1708–1709, when birds fell from the air. Firewood failed to burn. Cattle died. Rivers froze over. Saliva congealed before hitting the ground. Vineyards froze. Hunger abounded.

The minister's animated story was only casually received, until he raised his voice and hands and repeatedly shouted that the freeze had been a curse from God. Almost screaming, the minister continued his tirade with verses from the Bible that spoke of a coming darkness.

> *I will darken the earth in the clear day.* (Amos 8:9, KJV).
>
> *Let their eyes be darkened, that they see not.* (Psalms 69:23, KJV)"

After some minutes of endless gibberish, and when passengers showed expressions of weariness, the boatsman asked for assistance to seat the minister, implying a protocol of safety. When some adults lurched to quieten the minister and return him to his seat, and when his wife stood to accommodate the men, she suddenly fell into the frigid current behind the fast-moving scow.

Two days after the fatal incident, the minister again stood in the boat, with passengers anticipating a remorseful apology for his earlier outburst. Instead, he raised his voice again, screaming that God would chasten every immigrant in Rotterdam and send a curse on their journey at sea. He immediately joined his wife.

Some found the minister's blabbering frightening, leading them to reconsider leaving their homeland. While the tirades did not rattle the

Grindstaffs, they privately acknowledged the possibility of religious fanatics onboard.

As days on the river passed with little to do but sit idly in the scow, the attention of some men occasionally turned to young Anna, sitting timidly beside her sheltering parents. Most men seemed to be in control of their boredom and lust, except for two men traveling together, probably in their early twenties. The most vocal one was called "Frog" by his companion, called "Nit." Their crude character often surfaced with unwanted compliments towards Anna, amid suggestions that her parents were sheltering her.

Nit had a habit of mimicking portions of Frog's speech, giving assurance that he was strongly second in command. Both men wore clothing that was tattered and baggy, with Nit's trousers ending just above his ankles. Both had unkempt shoulder-length hair. The stain on the Frog's upper front teeth revealed a noticeable wide separation.

Frog regularly made taunting remarks to the parents, followed by flirtatious laughter directed towards Anna, then turning and winking to those nearby for approval. However, the lengthy stares from passengers suggested that they were offended by the bullies.

Passengers maintained their calm demeanor despite frequent pestering from Frog and Nit, until one morning when a tall man named Tugal (aka Tug) occupied a seat near Anna. He was about seven

21

feet tall—a head or so taller than most others on the boat—and appeared to be in his forties.

Veseevis (Ve-see-vis) Switzler, a traveling companion, appeared to calm Tug's temperament by gently resting a hand on one arm, just above a reddening clenched fist. Tug looked to be struggling with mental health issues, or at least his facial expression indicated a temper-control problem. The morning sun on his glittering blue eyes gave the appearance of near-sobbing, but later encounters revealed that he always appeared tearful, regardless of any emotional stimulus.

Frog resumed his unwelcome remarks toward Anna and her parents after observing that Veseevis had repressed Tug's emotions.

However, the nagging abruptly ended two days later when a young man approached Anna's parents and identified himself as Johann (John) Goines. Anna stood, and they immediately hooked arms as if old friends. Frog's nagging stopped after Johann crowded into the seat beside Anna, presumably because of Johann's strong authoritative voice.

A scheduled boat change at a toll station prevented Frog and Nit from continuing their journey because funds arrived from an unknown source to pay the boatman to transfer them to another boat. Later rumors circulated that the bullies were suspected militia deserters who had paid their fare to Rotterdam with money from a robbery.

With Frog and Nit off the boat, the passengers enjoyed sunny days together, sharing stories about their backgrounds and personalities. During a long stop at a toll station (the stations deliberately created delays to sell more products), Uncle Barth learned much about Tug from his friend Veseevis: that Tug's parents had died a few years apart, leaving him alone in his country home. Veseevis took in Tug but as a young man, he left for glitz and glitter in a distant city. Tug returned to Veseevis' house about a year later after suffering a head injury and trauma from a robbery. Tug never fully recovered, and the incident left him a quieter person. He withdrew into silence, rarely speaking.

Before departing for America, Tug had spent his days near Zweibrucken working with Veseevis, creating little wooden clock pieces. Veseevis had previously worked as an apprentice for a cuckoo clock maker in the Black Forest region before relocating close to Zweibrucken to be farther from France.

The Crisis at Rotterdam

Immigrants loudly celebrated at the midday
sight of Rotterdam Harbor after weeks in cramped
Rhine boats on the winding river. The century-old
fishing village was alive with activity. Small vessels
bobbed in favored locations for the daily haul.
Seagulls made precision dives for food, and country
folk carted their possessions from the city along the
riverbank pathway. The sudden pitching of the stern
and aft gave some poor souls reason to heave
overboard.

In 1738 the city population of 40,000
continued to serve as a starting point for many
immigrants sailing to America. For a few years, the
enormous migrations appeared to depopulate

portions of the Palatinate, which encompassed the Rhineland Pfalz, the Rhineland Palatinate, and a portion of Baden. One estimate placed the exodus at over 100,000, given the substantial German-speaking population in Pennsylvania during the early 1700s.

Uncle Barth, who had been impatiently waiting to vacate the boat, departed quickly for the bustling city with his characteristic swinging of arms, confident of pleasurable encounters. Barth was one of those "first-in-line" types, while Michael's father had a "wait-and-see" personality. Barth anticipated a passing view of their awaiting ship, fresh food, a brief tour of the city before embarkation, clean clothes, and perhaps a small gathering with fellow countrymen. Those fantasies were never realized.

As crowds passed by the harbor vessels, someone asked, "Where are the big ships?" Everyone was saddened upon learning that the ships had not arrived.

The flood of immigrants quickly caused a crisis among Rotterdam officials, fearing a disease epidemic or the potential for abandoned children to become wards of the state. City officials promptly relocated the immigrants to the ruins of St. Elbert's Chapel, which was located about two miles outside the city, near Kraligen.

City merchants and ship captains exploited the restricted immigrants. The ongoing bargaining and purchasing activities outside the city further depleted the meager resources of many impoverished migrants.

Due to the scarcity of labor, ship commanders actively sought out the healthiest immigrants for their vessels. In 1738, a record sixteen ships would undertake the crossing, compared to an average of five ships for each of the previous ten years.

Hypothetically, if all ships were of the flute design (which, according to Culver, would require no more than 10–15 men), a minimum of 50–75 mariners per year would have been required for the average five ships prior to 1738. However, if the sixteen ships in 1738 were flutes, the labor requirement would have ranged from 160 to 240 seamen. Therefore, because ship designs other than flutes were used for the 1738 crossing, qualified ship labor would be in short supply.

All manner of bargaining was on the table between ship captains and impoverished families. An agreement was reached to waive fares for the member of a deceased member if death occurred before the halfway point of the journey. The captain would be responsible for the deceased. This was done to address the concerns of elderly and ill travelers who were concerned about their safety at sea.

Rotterdam's city fathers quickly realized the difficulty of regulating immigration traffic. The unpredictability of ship availability, the scarcity of available living accommodations, health risks, and other logistical obstacles forced leaders to establish provisions outside the city in tents and makeshift structures. City leaders privately acknowledged a need to "get them out of the way." (Wikipedia, Hope & Co., footnote 7)

De Hoogstraat te Rotterdam-A black and white drawing of a city street. Public Domain image of Netherlands landscape, 17ᵗʰ-18ᵗʰ century cityscape, free to use, no copyright restrictions image Picryl description.

Gif Teed

The Grindstaffs fared well in Rotterdam during the wait for ships to arrive, sheltering in an empty warehouse while working in a nearby laundry. Two brothers, "Forney" and "Pos", who worked for their demanding father operated the steamy, rank-smelling backstreet business. The brothers wheeled in soiled laundry for cleaning and supervised transients who were willing to work.

Behind his back, some laundry workers occasionally called him "Fat Forney." Young Michael received a sharp rebuke from his parents for voicing the slur. On a second occasion, my father (Nichel) administered a memorable physical punishment.

The Grindstaffs were faithful hard workers at the laundry and especially thankful that their employment enabled personal laundry needs, and was within walking distance of their shelter. Because of their dedicated work, a bond of friendship developed between the Grindstaffs and the two brothers.

Affluent customers enabled the laundry business to greatly prosper. The uniformed brothers rolled soiled laundry for deluxe service through the impressive front entrance. The clean and press deluxe service was delivered in coffin-shaped bamboo chests with bronze latches. However, routine service consisted of dropping off numbered sacks with drawstrings at a small side window.

36

The grumpy owner of the laundry coached a small black male named Gif Teed, who was about ten years old, to regularly stroll the work areas and loudly play raspy sounds on his harmonica wherever he spotted idle workers. He seemed a lonely child, hardly ever speaking. The screeching harp, however irritating, stirred the distant owner to soft chuckling. However, without explanation, the owner oftentimes struck Gif Teed with a short whip, leaving marks on his arms and back, but he quickly recovered and cradled the child as if nothing had happened.

Gif Teed was little more than tolerated by Forney and Pos, who sometimes sensed a strained relationship, especially when their father smiled with delight and called the child "Giftee", vaguely displaying favoritism. However, Forney and Pos restrained their jealousies, content to quietly pocket the gratuities from wealthy customers.

Michael's parents anticipated they would become indentured upon arrival in Philadelphia despite their frugalness and long working hours in the laundry. Their outlook was hardly surprising because of their many expenses down the Rhine and the exorbitant prices within the city. Many other migrants shared the same fate. Ship captains handled the indentures straightforwardly, receiving compensation from the bidder in Philadelphia. The Grindstaffs hoped for plantation work in the Carolinas, but most importantly they wanted the family to be together. Although Michael's family

38

spent long hours in the laundry, they rarely missed a

day strolling to the seaport to see if any ships had

arrived.

The Immigration Ships of 1738

The *Rotterdam Courant* reported on June 22 that British shipping merchants provided and hastily outfitted five ships from the Hope Shipping Firm. These were *Queen Elizabeth, Thistle, Oliver, Winter,* and *Glasgow.*

Uncle Barth dashed to the *Thistle*, evoking a Biblical image of Lot sprinting from Sodom. Most immigrants had endured enough of Rotterdam. Many were farmers who desired to reach Philadelphia and trudge beyond carnal city life to the untamed frontier.

However, some immigrants stayed in Rotterdam. Whether destitute or weary, some Palatines adapted to the bustling street markets and crowded living quarters, the constantly changing traffic, the cluttered docks, the language barriers, the fraudulent deceptions, the sleazy prey on children, the degrading humiliation of confinement, and the not-so-secret world of slave trafficking.

Although the sight of the Hope and Company ships lifted spirits, voyagers soon got a glimpse of the onboard crowding they would experience for months at sea. In 1738, several factors led to the loading of vessels above capacity:

1. There was not only a shortage of ships for the sixteen crossings, but importantly a significant demand for trained mariners, likely over 200% since only five average crossings were made in previous years. Overloading would have been a digressionary judgement in the face of shipping and labor shortages.

2. Some ships did not count children.

3. Jewish slavery interests in Rotterdam expressed a desire to "get them (immigrants) out of the way," (Wikipedia's "Hope and Company," footnote 7.)

4. The Hope and Company's so-called "top years" (profit) for the transport of migrants to Philadelphia were *1738, 1744, 1753,* and 1765. Details in the Wikipedia reference, state that the 1738- top year, generated premium income, about $30 per passenger compared to about $6 per passenger in off years. Over a long period (1600–1775), the passenger fare was about ten pounds sterling ($7), according to Grubb.

5. The Atlantic crossings were more economical if the vessels had more weight (ballast),

43

enabling quick voyages to the Americas and consequently quicker returns with valuable commodities.

The *Thistle* was not a passenger ship in the sense there were no individual rooms, no privacy, or reasonable accommodations. Most immigration ships were cargo vessels. They returned from the Americas, bringing tobacco, sugar cane, cotton, furs, lumber, pine tar, and other valuable commodities. Overloading with passengers on the return trip to the Americas mitigated any underutilized cargo space, which represented a diminution of profit.

Many cargo ships were of the Dutch fluyt (also known as flute) design, specifically designed for transporting cargo on transoceanic voyages. Culver, in his masterful work, stated that flute ships were generally three masted, approximately 80 feet in length, pear-shaped (when viewed from fore or aft), and weighing 200–300 tons. When the ships had three masts, they often rigged the rearmost (mizzen) mast with a triangular sail, while the front sails were square rigged. On the upper deck, some flutes carried canons, while the lower "deck" served as a cargo hold.

The "passenger" hold was not of normal human height; i.e., Tug could not walk upright. Simple block-and-tackling techniques required only 10 to 15 men to sail a flute, according to Culver. During the 17th century, the lower cost of transportation by flutes gave Dutch merchants a significant edge, resulting in the English adopting this design.

The publication "Pennsylvania German Pioneers" contains a comprehensive listing of the immigration ships that sailed between 1727 and 1775. Among the 324 ships that sailed during this period, the following additional designs were also included:

25 ships of Snow design

14 Brigantines

4 Brigs

11 Galleys

6 Bilanders

Bilanders were not designed for the Atlantic crossing, although one successfully crossed in 1738, while a second, the *Oliver*, sank.

The 324 ships had 193 captains, most of whom crossed the Atlantic once, but 46 crossed up to eight times. Culver's masterful work, "The Book of Old Ships," informs that "it is more than probable that many flutes crossed to America."

A Flute, 1677 (Weneeslas Hollar)__ the official

position taken by the Wikimedia Foundation is the

work is in the public domain because the author dies in

1677, so the work is in the author's life plus 100 years.

SHIP NAME	PASSENGERS	ARRIVAL IN PA
Catherine	15	July 27
Winter*	252	September 5
Glasgow*	349	September 9
Two Sisters	11	September 9
Robert & Alicer*	320	September 11
Queen Elizabeth*	324	September 16
Thistle*	300	September 19
Friendship	187	September 20
Nancy	150	September 20
Fox	95	October 12
Davy	121	October 25
Saint Andrew	300	October 27
Bilander Thistle	152	October 28
Elizabeth	95	October 30
Charming Nancy	200	November 9
Enterprise	120	December 6

*These five ships were made ready by the Hope & Co. on June 22.

The Hope & Company

Part A: The Shipping Business

In 1738, how could several thousand immigrants find economic accommodation in or near Rotterdam for weeks or months before shipping to America became available? And how could these Palatines, of whom many were impoverished, afford their fares?

These questions motivated this author to review the history of Hope & Co.

During the 1700s and 1800s, this Dutch company was one of several competing Atlantic shippers that significantly controlled the Philadelphia market. When the Palatines arrived in

Rotterdam in the spring of 1738 British merchants

quickly chartered ships from Hope Shipping to

provide transportation to America.

Six sons of Scottish merchant

Archibald Hope (1664–1743)—Archibald Jr.,

Isaac, Zachary, Henry, Thomas, and

Adrian—made fortunes from business

ventures around the world, dealing in

insurance, storage, and a dizzying array of

commodities. Three of the sons-Archibald Jr.,

Isaac, and Zachary made a profit for Hope &

Co. by transporting immigrants from

Rotterdam to Philadelphia. Their so-called

"top" (profit) years were 1738, 1744, 1753,

and 1765, when they received sixty guilders

per passenger, compared to eleven guilders in off years. According to footnote 7 of Wikipedia's Hope & Co. history, the city of Rotterdam and the local Mennonite Church allegedly paid for immigrant transportation. The strange title of footnote 7 is "Empty Contract Promises Will Be Without Guarantee in Heaven." A closer inspection of footnote 7 in the Hope & Co.'s Wikipedia provides a wealth of additional information.

Beginning of quote of footnote 7

"In this early period, the Hope brothers made money organizing shipments for Quakers out of Rotterdam (under the direction of Archibald Jr., Isaac, and Zachary) and the slave trade in Amsterdam (under the direction of Thomas and

Adrian). The top years for the Quaker transports to Pennsylvania were 1738,1744,1753 and 1765. These transports were paid for by the City of Rotterdam and the local Baptist Church (Mennonite Church stated earlier), since the Quakers had no money and the city needed to do something about the refugees. In top years the Hopes received 60 guilders per Quaker, and in off years 11 guilders per Quaker. Notice how the Jews paid to get rid of the Quakers/Refugees by funding their removal to Pennsylvania to get them out of the way. The slave trade was much less lucrative, but the care of the slaves on board the ships was worse. Of these, 16% died on board. During the Seven Years War (1756-1763) the Hope brothers became very wealthy from speculation."   End of quote, footnote 7

According to the mentioned Wikipedia document, footnote 7, the individual fare from Rotterdam to Pennsylvania in 1738 was around 60 guilders, or approximately $30 in American currency. [From about 1300 to 2002, the euro replaced the currency of guilders.] The Grindstaff family's fare would have been about $200 if not paid by the City of Rotterdam (Footnote 7).

Many immigrants who sailed to Philadelphia with Hope & Co. financing between 1736 and 1738 were destitute, classified as "leftovers," according to Grubb. This designation stemmed from the time-honored "have and have not" economic distinction. During the period 1736–1738, immigrants who sailed from Rotterdam to the American colonies on ships

other than those of Hope & Co. had money
for fare, or sponsorship, or an agreement to
servitude. Otherwise, Hope & Co. by default
transferred "leftover" immigrants. Grubb
noted that under these financial
circumstances, an immigrant received passage
from Hope & Co. through the redemptioner
servitude system.

Originating in Rotterdam, this flexible
redemptioner system allowed poor emigrants an
opportunity to find alternative ways of paying their
passage upon arrival in Philadelphia (if not free,
according to footnote 7), such as borrowing from
those already settled, or working for two to four
years. The combination of the redemptioner system

and strong immigrant preferences for Philadelphia may have appeared to give Hope & Co. a brief period of monopoly.

Part B: The Slavery-Related Business

Thomas and Adrian supervised the slavery-related business from Amsterdam, helping Hope & Co. become one of Europe's most successful companies. Around 1780, slavery-related enterprises, such as slave plantation financing and connected sugar, coffee, and diamond commerce, accounted for more than half of total earnings. During the period 1795-1815 Thomas' American nephew Henry Hope (1736-1811) ran the company, doing business with different countries, including Sweden, Poland,

Russia, Portugal, Spain, France, and the United States.

In 1804, the Hope & Co. issued shares to finance the Louisiana Purchase, thanks to negotiations by Henry Hope. This sale provided funds for Napoleon's wars. Native Americans occupied all the land, except New Orleans.

Part C: The Nexus between the Dutch Bank ABN AMRO and the Hope & Co.

Hope & Co. was a forerunner of this significant commercial bank, headquartered in Amsterdam. Historically, Hope & Co. had worked in cooperation with R. Mees& Zoonen until a merger in 1966 formed the Mees & Hope Bank, and this bank later became a historical progenitor of ABN AMRO after other mergers in 1996 and 2010.

In 2006 and again in 2020 the Dutch Bank ABN AMRO, conducted a thorough investigation into Hope & Co.'s past business links with plantation slavery. In these investigations this Dutch bank, ABN AMRO, revealed the Hope family's links to the slave trade.

The more recent 2020 ABN AMRO research report is unique in that, while it builds on the earlier study in 2006, the 2020 research is based on many hundreds of previously unexamined archival documents related to the Hope & Co. The Hope archive (1725-1940) is an important source for the history of Amsterdam and the Netherlands as the center of world commerce in the 18th century. In 1977 the archive was given to the Amsterdam city archives, where it is now open to the public (Footnote 7, the Hope & Co.).

The title of the 118-page commissioned research report is "Slave History of ABN AMRO's Historical Predecessors." The reading of this report is highly recommended to those seeking greater understanding of the Hope & Co.

It is not in this author's interest to explore the extensive slave-related activities of Hope & Co described in the 2020 research report, but rather to highlight salient findings from the ABN AMRO report, where these findings may relate to information presented in footnote 7 in the Wikipedia record of Hope & Co. The following is a list of this author's questions.

1. What was the meaning of "to get them out of the way"?

<u>Suggested answer by this author:</u>

The presence of so many immigrants in Rotterdam was possibly viewed as an inconvenience by some of the citizenry.

2. Who paid for getting them (immigrants) out of the way? Jews? The city of Rotterdam? Churches?

<u>Suggested answer by this author:</u>

Any of the three, or all three. Removing the immigrants, while seemingly expensive, may have been an investment to be rewarded by the gain of valuable commodities from the returning vessels to Europe from the Americas. It may be that only certain refugees would receive free fare, the "leftover" ones not able to pay their fare. The process for discerning these seems problematic. The expression "get them out of the way" may have been a narrow judgement on those "leftover" refuges having little resources.

3. Were there any Quaker immigrants who "had no money"? Were they Palatines?

<u>Suggested answer by this author:</u>

Most likely Palatine refugees.

4. Was Hope & Co.'s role of funding their removal to Philadelphia rather than to another province a convenient redemptioner solution?

The enormous profitably to the Hope & Co. and possibly some other shippers (445% upcharge in fare) favored the redemptioner system in Rotterdam, and perhaps allowed for digressionary "kickbacks" to whomever (Jews, churches, or others)

5. What was the context of including slave traffic and the 16% fatalities at sea in footnote 7?

Suggested answer by this author

If the discussion in Rotterdam centered around "getting them out of the way" at a 445% upcharge, then overloading of vessels may have been a temptation, especially if ships were not available. The mortality rate of 16% may have been a worst- case mortality.

65

It is impossible to calculate the impact of slave-produced goods returning from the Americas, no matter the cost of immigrant fares.

From Page 18- ABN AMRO REPORT

The Hope & Co. prospered during the period of slave trade. European markets welcomed the market goods brought from the Hope-financed slave plantations of the Americas. Amsterdam and Rotterdam played major roles for the colonial goods.

For example, during the Seven Years War between France and England (1756-1763), Hope & Co.'s returning ships generated more money than redemptioners did. While England and France were at war, the neutral Dutch Republic profited handsomely by supplying items from their own plantation possessions. Prior to the conflict, Thomas and Adrian Hope gave ten million guilders to the Amsterdam Exchange Bank, but Grubb notes their

66

contributions skyrocketed to 47 million guilders ($23.5 million) in 1762.

It is impossible to assess the earnings from the slavery-related companies of the Hope & Co., because the Hope's frequently serviced debts through trade, as illustrated by the following example from the ABN AMRO report.

"In a world without non-cash transfers, there were two ways to settle foreign financial transactions. The first was incredibly high-risk international transports of money or precious metals. The second way was to settle through international trade. This could be done by paying the creditor in merchandise, or by having a local intermediary pay out part of the trade proceeds to the creditor via a so-called bill of exchange. For Amsterdam trading and finance houses such as Hope & Co., this provided an additional, often forgotten connection to the slavery system. In the early nineteenth century, for example, Hope & Co. lent millions to the ailing Portuguese

67

Crown. The agreements between the company and Portugal specified that the loan would be paid largely in slave-mined diamonds from the Brazilian province of Minas Gerais and from the proceeds of trade in slave-produced tobacco, cotton, and brazilwood."

Part B.1 The Value of Slaves

Throughout the ABN AMRO report of 2020, there is a recurrent finding that slaves had a value depending on their positions on plantations, in addition to the value of products that they produced. In the 2020 ABN AMRO report, the plantation owner regarded an individual slave as providing no service unless their production or position demonstrated it.

From Page 59- ABN AMRO REPORT

"The valuation reports regularly received by Hope & Co. partners reveal the shocking truth that enslaved people were given an individual book value. Indeed, they were seen as production units and served as collateral for loans. However, the reports also reveal how important the work of specialized enslaved people was for plantation owners. One example is the valuation of the Jerusalem sugar

69

plantation on St. Croix in April 1776, a plantation with 145 enslaved people. An enslaved person on this plantation was given an average financial value of 357 pesos in the accounts. Those who practiced a craft were clearly valued the highest…carpenter- 1000 pesos, cooper- 900 pesos, distiller- 850 pesos, sugar cook- 800 pesos…. some were assigned a value at zero, with the additional remark "of no service."

From Page 55- ABN AMRO REPORT

"When a plantation served as collateral for a Hope Co. loan, that collateral consisted not only of land and building. The enslaved people who lived and worked on the plantations formed part of the collateral."

From Pages 33-34- ABN AMRO REPORT

The Hope's slavery-related activities were already developing during this early period. Between 1713 and 1750 the right was in the hands of the British South Sea Company. One client of the Hope brothers was Samuel Collitt, who traded enslaved people under license of the South Sea Company in Caracas, in present day Venezuela. In exchange for enslaved people, he mainly received cacao from Spanish planters. He then exported this product, via Curaco, to Amsterdam, where the Hopes acted as intermediaries. They took care of the sale of cacao in Amsterdam and also arranged for insurance for cacao and tobacco shipments. The Hopes had more slavery connections through the Caribbean in this period. The firm had representatives on Curaco and St. Eustatius and traded in, among other things, sugar, and tobacco. An important business partner was the Boston resident Thomas Hancock, with whom the Hopes traded through a mutual representative on St. Eustatius. One of the products traded was dyewood, from a British settlement in Honduras. In 1741 Hancock (see note below) ordered one of his captains to buy "eight or ten good negro slaves" on a

71

Caribbean Island such as St. Eustatius, to resell them in the Bay of Honduras. There he had to purchase dyewood, destined for Boston or Amsterdam, "to be consigned to Messrs. Thomas & Adrian Hope."

<u>Note from this author</u>: Thomas Hancock died childless in 1764, leaving his wealth to his nephew, American patriot John Hancock.

Part C: Deaths Aboard Slave Ships, 1700-1800

<u>From Page 18-</u> ABN AMRO REPORT

During the 100-year period, 6.5 million Africans were forced onto slave ships. Approximately 15%, or more than 900,000, did not survive the journey to the Americas.

Part D: Apologies For Slavery

ABN AMRO APOLOGY

Despite movements to abolish slavery, Hope & Company remained active in the slavery-related business until the end, 1863___ when slavery was abolished in the Netherlands. A public apology by ABN AMRO was made in 2022 for this past activity.

APOLOGY FROM DUTCH KING WILLEM ALEXANDER FOR COUNTRY'S ROLE IN SLAVERY (2/7/24)

www.bbc.com/news/world-europe-660

During his speech in Amsterdam, King Willem-Alexander conceded that the "monarchs and rulers of the House of Orange took no steps against [slavery]."

"Today, I'm standing here in front of you as your King and as part of the government. Today I am apologizing myself," he said. "Today, I am asking for forgiveness for the crystal-clear lack of action." Accompanied by his wife Queen Maxima, the King acknowledged that he could not speak for the entire nation, but he told the crowd that "the vast majority of Dutch citizens "do support the fight for equality for all people, regardless of colour or cultural background". (76562)

Reparations for Past Slavery Business by the Dutch

In June, a new study revealed that Dutch rulers received the equivalent of $595M in today's money between 1675 and 1770 from colonies where slavery was enforced.

On February 7, 2024, King Willem Alexander made a public apology for the Dutch role in slavery. Two years before King Willem-Alexander's apology, an article by Amara Amaryah (October 3, 2022) stated the Netherlands plan to pay $204 million in slavery reparations. The decision was made following the push of Black Lives Matter in the country.

The Prodigy

Descending below *Thistle's* deck, we located our small, assigned living area near overhanging lanterns. Since the *Thistle* was not a passenger ship, the below-deck hull was essentially a musty cargo hold. Rickety double-tier bunk beds pretty much defined the sleeping quarters.

Nichel faintly noticed a bamboo chest resembling the ones used by affluent customers at the laundry in Rotterdam. Two laundry workers had reportedly transported the chest onboard. Shipworkers in the vicinity were told that it contained an appreciation gift to the Grindstaffs, consisting of high-quality apparel that had been left at the laundry by forgetful and deceased customers.

Attempting to sit on the chest, Michael shouted that he heard music from inside. Barth rushed to the wiring on the latches and opened the lid, revealing a corpse-like Gif Teed holding his harmonica. The dazed stowaway slowly climbed over the side, lowered the lid, and sat down, playing beautiful music.

Gif Teed's appearance was dramatically sharper than it had been in the laundry house. He was not in his usual raggedly worn clothing, but decked out in an attractive orange knee-length coat and breeches. A close observation revealed a dainty silver necklace around his neck.

The emotionally stricken family gasped at the sight of Gif Teed and were dumbfounded by musical sounds they had never heard before—never in Hornbach. Leaning forward, Barth cautiously circled and eyed the young musician. Within minutes, the music echoed inside the cavernous hull, drawing curious crowds to the performance. Some of the older women began to grin, some to weep. Some reverently laid a coin beside the wingless cherub, as if a divine visitor. With professional deftness, Gif Teed hardly missed a musical note before sweeping up each coin and returning a childlike smile of thanks.

The Grindstaffs privately concluded that Gif Teed must remain with the family because of concern that a crime of abduction might be charged, even if it were feasible to return him to the laundry, in which case they also contemplated the possibility of the *Thistle* sailing without them.

A lesser concern was how the ten-year-old child was able to play beautiful music without any apparent training, despite being coached to produce only screeching noises to lazy workers in the laundry house. What was the cause of the child's failure to perform soothing music at the laundry house? The Grindstaffs had never encountered a prodigy.

Gif Teed was capable of articulating words during his early days with the

Grindstaffs, but he never spoke much, and only then in simple sentences. His evident suppression in the laundry house was interpreted as the cause of any speech deficiency. However, Barth was not satisfied that Gif Teed's early life was fully known, and raised questions about the silver necklace about the child's neck.

Others on the *Thistle* always welcomed the little prodigy, who daily roamed about the ship, though his home was with the Grindstaffs, with whom he ate and slept. His padded bed was in the bamboo laundry chest, into which he had been rolled onboard the ship by the jealous brothers, Forney, and Pos.

Contrary Winds

And when we had launched from thence, we sailed under Cyprus, because the winds were contrary.
(Acts 27:4, KJV)

The two immigration ships, *Thistle,* and *Oliver*, made contrasting voyages in 1738. Each left Rotterdam for America on June 22. The Hope Brothers owned each. Although the *Oliver*, a bilander, was smaller at 120 tons, each carried as many as 300 passengers. At sea, the two ships experienced contrasting voyages—the *Oliver* encountered fierce destructive winds while the *Thistle* was often slowed by light breezes.

Both the *Oliver* and *Thistle* had barely left Rotterdam on June 22, when, according to the June

24 edition of the *Rotterdam Courant*, a fierce storm forced a layover at Hellevoetsluis, a small coastal town just across from Goeree-Overflakke Island, south of Rotterdam. While docked at Hellevoetsluis, Captain William Walker and several passengers refused to return to the *Oliver*, fearing it was overloaded. Captain William Wright replaced Captain Walker.

While the *Thistle* was forced to layover at Cowes, the Grindstaff families became troubled about the nature of inspections that might take place while there, fearing the presence of a small black child would raise questions about how he had come to be in their company. Whether right or wrong, he was never allowed to be seen by inspectors who came below deck, because Michael sat on the smelly laundry chest making irritating sounds on a harmonica.

Inspections required by British navigation laws amounted to examining cargo, restocking some provisions if available, making repairs, and in some instances dealing with runaway passengers. In December 1737, thirty Palatines on the ship *Three Sisters*, sailing between Rotterdam and Cowes, ran away to England due to bad treatment and starvation rations.

Like the ship *Oliver*, severe weather hindered the *Thistle* while leaving Cowes, requiring it to shelter at Plymouth. The limping Captain Wilson seemed to take the delay in stride without an excessive display of emotion. His graying hair and stern voice were a testament to his years at sea. The captain was not inclined to be overly social with passengers, and interreacted with his crew as seemed necessary. An exception was daily interactions between Captain Wilson and the wandering Gif Teed.

After repairs, the *Oliver* sailed across the vast Atlantic towards America in early August, two months behind schedule. The depletion of food and fresh water became critical, whether due to inadequate supplies before departure, or layovers, or demands of the large passenger load. Fifty of the 300-plus passengers died, most of whom were children.

Grieving parents watched as their children were lowered into the deep.

Thirteen storms battered the *Oliver* during the crossing, one of which broke a mast. Both Captain Wright and his first mate died. Francis Sinclair was made captain.

A story in the November 24 issue of the *Virginia Gazettes* stated that the *Oliver* and another ship had passed by each other.

On January 3, 1739, the *Oliver* dropped anchor at the south end of Chesapeake Bay, Virginia. It was there that some passengers, overcome with hunger and dehydration, started a mutiny, demanding a boat to find any fresh water or food in a timely manner. A weather front prevented their return to the *Oliver*. The stranded mutineers observed powerful winds dragging the *Oliver* into a sandbar, greatly damaging the sinking ship's hull. Fifty drowned. About two hundred got off the ship, but the cold January water and cold nights took about 120 of the 200.

Carlo Toriano was one of *Oliver's* wreck survivors. In July 1739, the Hope Brothers asked him to say something positive about his trip. The Hope Brothers sent the request to Toriano to "build a case" in the event of a law suit that might accuse the *Oliver* as reason for the disaster. Carlo omitted the negative aspects of his speech, such as the overcrowding and the passengers' hunger and thirst.

He even wrote, "We sailed happily." People think he only said that stupid thing because the Hopes paid for his flight back to Switzerland. On November 24, 1739, the *Virginia Gazette* and several northern newspapers covered the *Oliver* tragedy.

Hindered by light winds at Plymouth the *Thistle* experienced both decreasing galley rations and grumbling passengers. Thankfully, there was a fair abundance of non-perishables, such as beans, grains, and peas, but some bread showed both mold and worms, and rodents had burrowed into some salt pork. Some passengers were gambling for essentials. Now, at mid-summer, the prospect of arriving in Philadelphia before late fall seemed a challenge.

Despite the light sailing winds, the passengers persistently demanded that Captain Wilson continue the voyage to the promised land. Boredom gripped the 300 grumblers confined to the eighty-foot vessel.

Wilson's bored crewmen offered no encouragement to the passengers. The 1738 sailing season had 16 ships crossing the Atlantic, whereas the average was five ships during each of the previous ten year. The increased number of ships led to a shortage of qualified personnel. Most of the present motley crew had never labored on anything larger than a bilander along the canals. Some crewmen were miserable failures, having spent hours in taverns. The pastime of some was spent in idleness, boxing, and wagering. Conversely, young Palatine males emerged as some of the best workers.

Faced with only light winds Wilson reluctantly gave orders to trim the sails against the gentle breeze and proceed toward the open sea. The *Thistle's* location from the previous day was nearly visible as it floated for days. With only light gusts present, the deck became unbearably heated, sending many passengers and crew to the on-deck cooling showers supplied by ocean water.

Because of the downtime for inspections at Cowes, the Grindstaff families were able to address some of their linguistic concerns. When the party of six departed Zweibrucken in 1738, they listed Cransdorf as their surname.

"Gohn of Rimschweiler, Fredrick Cromer of Rimschweiler, Barthel Cransdorf, Nickel Cransdorf, of that place, all six with their wives and children to America— *List of Emigrants from Zweibrucken,* September 19, 1738, ship *Thistle.*"

In the laundry at Rotterdam, their native-spoken surname from Hornbach and nearby Zweibrucken was mixed and expressed in various dialects. At Cowes, the Grindstaff became an accepted and pleasant-sounding surname.

The Sea Market

A party atmosphere quickly developed on the deck of the *Thistle* as it glided with soft winds from Plymouth Harbor. Fiddle playing and dancing lasted late into warm summer evenings. People devoured dry staples with a sense of abundance. The frivolity would last for eleven days.

During the eleven days, the sale and trade of personal items was a popular event. From sunup to late evenings, bargain hunters crowded the deck, socializing and securing choice items. Captain Wilson welcomed the daily events because personal coins were put into circulation, which eventually went for storeroom purchases. He likely favored the "Sea Market" because it silenced bored grumblers.

The market offered the following items for sale:

- Used clothing, shoes, boots, and hats
- Homemade wooden toys for children
- Musical instruments
- Some primitive cuckoo clocks and parts
- Pastes and potions for different ailments
- Old tools (mallets, axes, shears, etc.)
- Keepsakes from the home country
- Items borrowed at Rotterdam
- Box lots of various knives
- Kruger's "health food candy"
- Box lots of used candles from Rotterdam
- Nice treasures from dead people.
- There are three sets of intricately lidded chamber pots.
- Many bundles of rags and quilting materials
- An assortment of Bibles
- Two pairs of hands-free eyeglasses
- Nice bedding pallets for four
- Several chests, some damaged
- Miscellaneous gold items, including teeth
- Two small iron stoves
- Assortment of buttons
- Pewter containers
- Cooking utensils
- A variety of hand scythes
- Candles from Rotterdam

On the second day of the festive period Tug set up a shoe cobbler business on the rear aft deck. His demeanor while on the Rhine had suggested a mild mental impairment, but here on the sunny deck, he repaired the shoes and leather goods of others as one them.

However, Tug never smiled. He plied his trade with limited tools—some old leathers, some awls, and a very crude-looking shoe last. Captain Wilson and the ship carpenter, impressed by Tug's abilities, added to his inventory of tools on condition that he repair some sails. Whether out of admiration or pity, Wilson was occasionally seen staring at Tug.

Gif Teed danced joyfully onto the cobbler's work area on the second day of the Sea Market, gliding as if on ice, performing lively gigs on his harmonica. The prodigy's precision movements on the old deck were acquired from Pos at the laundry house in Rotterdam. Pos had frequently demonstrated his glides to arouse envy in his oversized brother. The dance-like movements were believed to be an early form of German clogging, characterized by the rhythmic coordination of elevating each knee and alternating ankle movements.

As audiences gathered to applaud Gif Teed's performances, Tug's work area near the dance floor became a drop-off location for leather repairs.

The cobbler occasionally cast an upward look at Gif Teed, but never smiled. Crowds became ecstatic when the lad alternated a brief shuffling dance and foot stomp into his performance, elevating his long, skinny arms above his head and self-applauding to the cheering crowd. Captivated by the crowd while he played his harmonica, the prodigy's brief interludes inspired some to cast coins at his feet.

Gif Teed skillfully swooped up the loose coins with eagle-eye vision as part of his performance. The spontaneous jubilation indicated that many of the spectators had long suppressed their opportunity for humor. An eruption of laughter and handclapping occurred when older stoics, shuffled their legs to dance, while fighting off arthritic restraints.

A bond developed between Tug and Gif Teed on *Thistle's* deck. Something missing from each life seemed to draw one to the other. Tug's watery eyes appeared more tearful when Gif Teed came near and played a melodic piece for him.

Their bond became stronger during the eleven days of Sea-Market, with Tug often seen carrying Gif Teed on his shoulders, so that all eyes marveled at the musical giant. A faint smile on Tug's face hinted the presence of conjoined personalities. Holding his harmonica in one hand, Gif Teed flashed his white teeth and waved his hat like a politician. The tricorn hat, a gift from the Sea

Market, boasted an orange hue with a black trim around the brim, which extended into the three corners. His dainty silver necklace, though barely noticeable, had been around the child's neck since his first appearance on the Thistle.

During the Sea Market, John Coon and Anna sneaked into a secluded area on deck for intimate moments, accompanied by young Michael. Their escape initially turned out to be the entryway to the not-so-private community cooling shower stalls.

In their search for privacy, John and Anna wandered upon a tattered sunshade where an aged fortuneteller sat, unsuccessfully drumming up business. Curiously, they inquired about their

99

future, content that it was simply a matter of having fun together. John and Anna eagerly embraced following the fortuneteller's prediction of a large family, blessing their future marriage. However, the wrinkled old lady paused briefly before concluding that their marriage would experience sorrow. Michael trailed behind the departing couple, picking up the sad final words about their future

Euroclydon

After eleven blistering days of Sea Market thrills, the *Thistle* sailed northeast with favorable winds and gathering clouds. As evening fell, the crowds gathered their treasures and headed to familiar, dim, and smelly quarters. Many had occasionally slept on deck, exchanging stories with friends during the warm nights.

Before retiring below, an unfamiliar young man gained much attention by calling for a prayer of thanksgiving and guidance for the sailing days ahead. Captain Wilson appeared to have accepted his self-invitation in advance, as evidenced by their brief encounter. Some passengers began to walk away when his supposedly brief prayer seemed like a dissertation.

However, heads turned towards the young man when he compared the current voyage to that of the beloved Apostle Paul, who was sailing to Rome. Paul had warned that prevailing soft winds would turn into a fierce storm, which would cause much loss, but some materialistic passengers ignored Paul's warnings.

> *But not long after, there arose against it (the ship) a tempestuous wind, called Euroclydon. And when the ship was caught up and could not bear into the wind, we let her drive.* (Acts 27:14,15, KJV)

Tired listeners ignored Wilson's weatherman, dismissing any parallel between the

Biblical event and the present voyage. Cynical minds agreed that the young man, though pleasant in appearance, lacked scientific credibility to predict a euroclydon-like event. Indeed, they boasted the weather had been wonderful.

As he walked slowly to his cabin a few seasoned sailors overheard Captain Wilson discussing cyclonic storms, which can sometimes develop in winds blowing from northeast to southeast at certain times of the year, sometimes in the Mediterranean, and lasting for up to fifteen days.

Wilson had gained knowledge from other sea captains who were familiar with the fierce autumn winds known as gregales. The captain's self-rehearsal suggested that he was not as dismissive of the young man as were some of the doubting passengers.

Tug came alongside the fair-complexioned clairvoyant after many had descended below deck. Any conversation was likely one-sided because Tug seldom spoke.

Exhausted revelers from the withering sun trimmed their lanterns before retiring, while others simply dropped onto their lice-infected pallets. The sound of breaking waves, like gentle rain, brought on sleepy coziness.

However, waves soon pounded onto the deck above, disrupting peaceful sleep. No one was prepared for the churning sea gales, whose waves

seemingly rose like mountains and tumbled over the

ship, causing fear of going down into the deep. The

dark cavern echoed with pitiful crying and prayers.

Strong waves pounded the starboard side, lifting

the ship and spiraling it counterclockwise to the top

of an apparent monster wave. Had we not lowered

the sails earlier, the vessel would have undoubtedly

rotated to its side and plunged into the deep. No one

dared to stand. Passengers were thrown into

neighboring spaces, falling over flimsy broken beds.

After climbing to perhaps 25 feet atop a

giant wave, the vessel let out a thunderous crack,

followed by a frightening downward glide. The

helmsman later alerted First Mate Tarp that the

ship's compass indicated that it had rotated northwest to southwest. Tarp, on the other hand, asserted that the ship's smashing motion may have affected the accuracy of the compass. Some cried aloud, fearing that the ship was breaking apart due to a prolonged grating noise inside the bottom hull, but someone in the darkness suggested that the noise might be the result of moving ballast, adding that ship laborers had added more ballast stones while berthed at Rotterdam.

The Grindstaffs, scattered as they were, found a lantern to locate the bamboo chest where Gif Teed had made his bed. To their amazement, they discovered Tug on the floor, holding onto the chest.

After several nights of smaller whipping gales, the seas became calm. Daylight offered escape to the deck and desperate relief from the disgusting smell of the living quarters.

First Mate Tarp opined that a euroclydon event had not occurred, but rather the development of rogue waves in the North Sea, directed between the Carolina coast and Bermuda. Tarp did not appear to have many believers, who recalled that Tarp had earlier seemed critical of the young psychic.

Captain Wilson refrained from saying much about the violent nights at sea, apparently desiring to calm the most fearful.

Some people, who had cynically ignored the warning from the young seer, gathered to search for him and inquire about the source of his knowledge. However, they were unable to locate him and concluded that he had perished during the storm. Tug's watery-like eyes seemed to indicate that he was distraught upon hearing of the young man's disappearance.

Tarp showed greater concern over the absence of one of the three rat dogs that normally roamed the ship, as if to dismiss the importance of the clairvoyant. Ship laborers valued the dogs, likely of the Schnauzer breed, for their ability to control the rodent population, a common problem on grain-carrying ships. The missing dog was never found.

It seemed appropriate to offer prayers of thanksgiving on the deck for divine deliverance from the terrible storm. Most of the people gathered near the stern to listen to Captain Wilson read the following scripture, which was followed by a prayer.

They that go down to the sea in ships, that do business in great waters; These see the works of the LORD, and his wonders in the deep. For he commandeth, and raiseth up the stormy wind, which lifteth up the waves thereof. They mount up to the heaven, they go down again to the depths: their soul is melted because of trouble. They reel to and fro, and stagger like a drunken man, and are at their wit's end. Then they cry unto the LORD in their trouble, and he bringeth them out of their distresses. He maketh the storm a calm, so that the waves thereof are still. Then are they glad because they be quiet; so he bringeth them unto their desired haven.
(Psalms 107:23-30, KJV)

The comfort of the scripture was short-lived when Tarp learned that lowering the sails, however incomplete, had allowed the storm to send the *Thistle* southward. We would spend days recovering the original course.

Kruger's Candy

While Captain Wilson was reading Psalms 107, admirers noticed his apparent mimicking of the verse: "They reel to and fro and stagger like a drunken man." Perhaps some admirers thought Captain Wilson was adding drama to the scripture reading, but any thoughts of role-playing ended when their captain collapsed to the deck.

First Mate Tarp ordered nearby officers to carry Wilson to his cabin, barking with an authoritative tone that he had never enjoyed.

Captain Wilson's lifeless body gave some observers reason to whisper whether death was near, sighing that their captain had experienced much stress in recent days.

However, within three days, Captain Wilson stirred from his near-death state and drank small amounts of wine with cheese. Acting Captain Tarp had taken temporary leadership of the *Thistle*, but Wilson quickly resumed control once he recovered.

Twelve older men had died while their captain looked to be approaching death, all showing indications of frailty and a rapid heartbeat like their leader. Several older females were in a weakened condition. Fear spread throughout the *Thistle*.

When Captain Wilson had sufficiently recovered, he held an officers' meeting at his court on deck. Ignoring the courtside yellow flag, anxious crowds pressed closer to the open-air court. [A yellow flag signified that Captain Wilson was meeting with his officers in a restricted area; a blue flag indicated that court was in session.]

Normally, the open-air court was held once a week, weather permitting, in the designated area, which was surrounded by a wooden banister on three sides, approximately three feet high. A simple bench was located inside the banister area, facing Captain Wilson's elevated table. To maintain control, two or three officers positioned themselves at the forefront of the court. Spectators watched proceedings from a marked distance.

The court proceedings began with an inquiry into common activities that took place before, during, and after the recent storms but quickly shifted focus to the foods consumed. The inquiry revealed that many had not eaten much during the storms but added that during the eleven days of Sea Market, they consumed Kruger's candy due to its sweet and satisfying flavor, which served to avoid the need for food from below deck. Suddenly, the crowd erupted in loud voices, shouting, "Kruger's candy, Kruger's candy!" The two words swiftly became a deafening tribal chant.

Wilson gazed downward, realizing that he had been consuming the popular black drop on a regular basis in recent days. He recalled the numerous occasions when Kruger had presented him with personal samples at the Sea Market. The small black candy droplets had frequently served as a delicious alternative to a trek to the cabin for cheese or beans.

Judge Wilson immediately ordered his officers to locate and bring Kruger to court for potential criminal activity.

Crowds surrounded Kruger and chanted his name as officers raised the blue flag and led the detested "Candyman" into court. Numerous criminal proceedings had transpired in Judge Wilson's court, including theft, gossiping, intoxication, lewdness, fighting, adultery, and nighttime disturbances.

However, the court had never recorded any actions that led to the death of another passenger.

Kruger sprang to his feet when Judge Wilson inquired about the source of the candy drops and the reason for tainting the candy to cause such suffering. Kruger loudly insisted that he had not tainted the candy and went on to declare its purity.

With clenched fists raised, the crowd loudly chanted "tainted" again and again. After ordering Kruger to his seat, Judge Wilson requested an explanation of his activities in Rotterdam, which could potentially affect the current criminal case. Kruger responded that during his weeks in Rotterdam, he had been employed in a low-end restaurant, where he welcomed both city workers and locals for a meal and social interaction. His primary responsibilities included receiving and cleaning produce and meat, as well as cleaning the kitchen and tables. In exchange for his work, he received free boarding in a storage room and portions of leftover food from the kitchen.

When Judge Wilson pressed for additional information concerning his role of welcoming customers, Kruger acknowledged that an additional duty was to provide a complimentary black candy drop at the customer entrance door as well as on customer tables. The small, delicious treat was more than just sweet. According to Kruger, many customers believed the candy had beneficial effects on human health, for example, control of coughing, digestion (reflux), constipation, and anxiety control. According to Kruger, the small black drops were a common yet somewhat addictive treat in the city.

When Judge Wilson asked how he had acquired such a large quantity of the candy, Kruger confessed that he had stolen one of several large storage containers and had skimped on complementary samples, revealing his plans to pursue sales during his voyage. Kruger's scheme was to provide a complementary sample at sea, followed by a good-for-your-health sales pitch.

Having told his story, Kruger emphasized there was nothing tainted about the candy and that it was a favorite of both children and adults in Rotterdam. At this juncture, Kruger reminded Judge

Wilson of Gif Teed's frequent visits to the captain, supposedly for a sample.

Judge Wilson became silent, his facial expression indicating that this reminder had disturbed him. Judge Wilson sheepishly asked the crowd whether Kruger was guilty or innocent, and the majority repeatedly screamed "guilty." The circumstantial nature of the deaths rendered a hanging offense unjustified. However, emotions were high due to fears that others might also die.

Judge Wilson sentenced Kruger to 25 lashes at the post for his circumstantial involvement in the deaths and sufferings. Furthermore, Judge Wilson ordered Kruger to return all proceeds from his sales to the affected widows. Finally, Judge Wilson pronounced Kruger an outcast while on the *Thistle*, meaning that only minimum interactions with others should occur.

Kruger had no one to litigate his actions. The crowd had ruled against any possible innocence. If historians had been there, they could have told the angry crowd about the long history of the so-called "black drop" (black licorice), including how Hippocrates recommended it for treating ulcers in 400 BC, how King Tutankhamun hid a prized travel pack full of it in his tomb, how Alexander the Great and Julius Caesar gave it to their soldiers on long marches to keep them hydrated, and how Napoleon ate it all the time while fighting, until his teeth turned black.

It might have been different for Kruger in his case with Judge Wilson if there had been a trustworthy doctor there to tell the judge about all the researched health benefits of licorice, such as its ability to help with throat, kidney, stomach, dental, and mental health problems.

Most importantly, in an era of modern medicine, Kruger's case would have faced scientific scrutiny due to the abundance of literature on the potential risks now associated with the excessive consumption of black licorice

For example, the following article by Diane Calello, executive medical director of the New Jersey Poison Control Center, based at Rutgers New Jersey

Medical School, discusses safe consumption of black licorice.

Beginning of article

This week (9/24/20), The New England Journal of Medicine reported that a man with a poor diet died of cardiac arrest after eating a bag-and-a half of black licorice for weeks. Black licorice is safe to eat in small amounts. The case in the journal involved excessive consumption with very limited diet otherwise.

However, it is important to realize that black licorice is more than just candy. It contains glycyrrhizin acid, which can cause swelling and high blood pressure and deplete potassium and other electrolytes that may cause a cardiac arrhythmia or arrest. Glycyrrhizin acid can be found in other foods, such as jelly beans and beverages for flavor.

There is not a specific "safe" amount, but people with high blood pressure or heart or kidney disease should avoid black licorice, which can worsen these conditions. For people over 40, the FDA says that more than two ounces a day for two weeks may be problematic and cause irregular heart rhythm or arrhythmia. People who are on medications or supplements that may be affected by licorice consumption should consult their doctor.

End of article

Research by Cloyd on the chemistry of licorice in humans, including suggested intake limits, adds clarity to the potential dangers of black licorice. Dr. Cloyd noted that licorice is formally designated as Glycyrrhiza glabra, and that glycyrrhizin acid has a mineralocorticoid-like influence on the body, which can modulate electrolyte and fluid equilibrium, chiefly by enhancing sodium reabsorption and promoting potassium excretion in the kidneys. This may result in a syndrome termed pseudo aldosteronism, characterized by sodium retention and potassium depletion (hypokalemia). Dr. Cloyd's article specifies a suggested upper consumption limit by the European Union of 100 mg per day, equivalent to 60-70 grams of crude plant.

124

Kruger's trial was sadly one-sided. Passions were hot. Companions had died from eating the black candy. Everyone was fearful. Kruger was declared guilty.

The Shark Feeding

Day after day, day after day
we struck nor breath nor motion
As idle as a painted ship
upon a painted ocean.

Water, water, everywhere,
and all the boards did shrink;
Water, water, everywhere,
nor any drop to drink.

The very deep did rot: O Christ!
that this should ever be!
Yea, slimy things did crawl with legs
upon the slimy sea.

(*The Rime of the Ancient Mariner*, Part 2—
Samuel Taylor Coleridge)

It didn't matter if an euroclydon had blown over or not, the storm still left a terrible smell below deck. The ship was severely damaged by the storms. A spline would be necessary to repair the fractures in the rear mast. Rips occurred when inexperienced sailors did not fully lower the sails before the storm. The water barrels were teeming with worms. The ballast was inspected for repositioning, and it was discovered that lazy sailors had dumped ship-waste into the ballast hold instead of overboard. The availability of potable water was low. In order to maintain personal cleanliness and lower fevers, the cooling shower stations on deck—which made use of ocean water—required some maintenance.

The Jewish interests in Rotterdam had referred to it as "getting them out of the way" (Hope

& Company, Wikipedia, footnote 7), and the *Thistle* was one of several cargo ships that were part of the ambitious plan to quickly remove the Palatines from the city. Because of decisions made in Rotterdam the ships were overloaded, leading to food shortages and hardships during the voyages.

A wide range of illnesses affected the Grindstaff family. Among many others, Uncle Barth spent two days and nights on the deck, suffering from stomach pain, hoping that fresh air would help. Living conditions within the cramped hull were near intolerable because of the high humidity.

Gif Teed appeared to be unaffected by illness, while some others died. He seemed immune to sickness' which devastated others. Occasionally, the family questioned his apparent immunity, whether it was because he was so cheerful, or just because he was always around other passengers.

The contamination of drinking water made the spread of illness much worse. Limited efforts we made to gather rainfall or heavy morning dew when possible.

Bread and salt pork were priced more by the ship's storekeeper compared to before the journey began. Beans, peas, and cheese were among the many dry goods found. Some passengers died from malnutrition, illness, or failing health despite the provision of partially molded bread.

A memorable committal service was held on the starboard side, next to the high aft portion of the *Thistle*, when over twenty witnesses sang an old hymn of the church in honor of two children and an adult male. As the bodies were reverently lowered into the sea, Gif Teed played a harmonica rendition of the same hymn, leaving a lasting impression. Barth later quizzed family members how Gif Teed was able to pick up the tune of the old song so perfectly. Barth was always inquisitive of Gif Teed's early childhood.

Some of the sailors in the area continued their sport of boxing during the committal service, so the service was far from solemn.

A frightful reminder from Anna's past occurred one sunny day while she was strolling on deck with young Michael. Approached from behind, she heard the sneering words, "Where's mommy and daddy?" Anna quickly turned, recalling the voices of

Frog and Nit, the two Rhine bullies who had harassed her daily. She immediately ran with Michael to the safety of friends, then to her family. However, Anna was too grown up to tell her parents of the encounter, and Michael kept silent.

Weeks later, while Anna was using a community cooling shower, Frog and Nit invaded her privacy. Her loud screams attracted many people to the area. Tug had been repairing sails nearby and ran towards the screams. Without thinking, he charged Frog with unrelenting bullish anger. However, out of nowhere, Frog slashed Tug in the arm with a long knife. Tug lunged forward again with giant hands shaped for choking Frog. However, the tall giant suffered a stab to his side.

Unfazed by his wounds, Tug lunged towards Frog, his mind seemingly clouded by anger. Tug was about to receive the upward thrust of Frog's knife when Gif Teed darted between the two, childishly hoping to protect his friend. But the knife's thrust passed through the neck of little Gif Teed, who fell to the deck.

When Gif Teed's friends rushed to the bloody scene, Frog ran, waving his knife, unaware that there was nowhere to hide. He climbed atop the stern, threatening anyone who dared come near, swearing, and cursing that he was ready to take others with him. Crowds gathered in a semicircle and stared upwards at Frog from a safe distance.

While Frog continued cursing and waving his bloody knife to the crowd, a sailor silently released a tightly secured rope that tensioned the rear mizzen sail to the free end of the horizontal wooden boom, with the other end swiveled to the rear mast. In an instant, the long boom swept across its horizontal plane, knocking Frog overboard.

With no apparent intention of rescue, Uncle Barth and curious observers rushed to the aft area, expecting to see the villain swallowed by the sea. However, it so happened that the *Thistle* was in warm waters, and a school of sharks was feeding from the ship's waste.

Observers watched the shark playfully remove the dangling limbs of the screaming man.

After staring downward for the longest time, the stunned watchers silently returned to the place where little Gif Teed lay.

During the night, a mass gathering of mourners held a memorial service on deck to honor Gif Teed. Some women had cleaned the young prince and draped him in a white garment, revealing only his once-smiling face. A large, full moon brightened the early night as processions continued. Admirers, touched by the life of Gif Teed, over-flowed the deck. Many shared unforgettable stories, which often ended in tears.

The white shroud caused some observers to whisper that the child may have been of biracial origin, but acknowledged that the brightness of the large overhead moon may have lightened his appearance.

Nit faced judgement at sunrise, after a night of restraint. Waiting crowds quietly gathered on the deck as Captain Wilson limped to the courtside seat over his watery jurisdiction. At the very moment that Judge Wilson assumed his seat, Nit fell to the deck, crying that he had only been a follower—someone duped, someone worthy of but a few stipes. Judge Wilson, seemingly oblivious to the pleas, raised his head and ordered that Nit be immediately hanged and allowed to follow Frog. Appointed sailors completed the sentence.

Following the public hanging, Frog and Nit's belongings were found to contain a large sum of money. Captain Wilson gave this money to the recovering Tug to establish a shoe cobbler business in Philadelphia.

Gif Teed's morning committal service followed a wake that lasted well into the night. The young prince was lowered into the deep in the bamboo chest in which he was brought aboard the *Thistle*. The Grindstaffs discovered a mysterious sum of money under the false bottom of the chest that was more than enough to cover their travel expenses.

The Mutiny

On a fall-like morning on August 9, witnesses to the wedding of Johann Gohn and Anna Grindstaff gathered on the rear deck of the *Thistle* when focus abruptly shifted to a distant ship. As the fog began to lift, Captain Wilson, the officiant, noticed the flagless schooner making her way through the water.

Captain Wilson's stern order to evacuate the deck transformed smiling faces into terrified ones. Rumors spread of a pirate ship.

Johann and Anna planned to begin their marriage on the *Thistle,* although happy parents had hoped the couple would wait until their arrival *in* Philadelphia.

Fear gripped passengers as they speculated the possibility of pirates selling healthy Palatines into slavery while slaughtering unhealthy ones. Many voiced opinions that the Pirates would be disappointed if they were seeking monetary valuables.

Captain Wilson expressed concern to First mate Tarp that the approaching ship didn't have an identifying flag, and mentioned the difficulty of spotting a double gun deck. Wilson stated that pirates often conceal their identity until at close range.

After three days of keeping 150-200 yards of distance from the shadowing vessel, most of the crew had begun to experience paranoia. Captain Wilson seemed certain the distant ship had nefarious intent and suspected their initial tactic was to cast fear on both his passengers and crew. Wilson was correct.

First Mate Tarp and two crewmen angrily approached Captain Wilson on August 13, demanding that the *Thistle* approach the ship in the hopes of obtaining supplies of food, water, and medical treatment. Arguments ensued. It may not be a pirate ship, Tarp argued, and living conditions on the Thistle had become unbearable. A mutiny began.

Wilson turned down the request because he was unwilling to risk losing his ship or his life. As the rest of the crew watched in confusion, the three mutineers took hold of their captain and secured him in his cabin. After restraining Wilson Tarp gave the order to maneuver the *Thistle* toward the flagless ship.

After just a few minutes of rerouting towards the shadowing ship, the *Thistle's* passengers rushed from below and wasted no time in overcoming the three mutineers for a trial of munity.

Wilson's immediate plans to separate from the shadowing ship remained unsuccessful. On the contrary, both kept moving in the same direction, as if tandemly linked. The *Thistle's* lack of weaponry ruled out distant combat, and the ragged crew would never survive a face-to-face battle.

Finally, Captain Wilson carried out a conspicuous committal service in view of the shadowing vessel, and flew a yellow flag over the *Thistle* to signify an onboard health condition. Five bags, made from ripped sails, were lowered into the sea, simulating the burial of deceased passengers. The shadowy ship turned away.

Years later an elderly Michael Grindstaff chuckled, stating the bags contained ballast stones.

Captain Wilson's private conversation with Tarp signaled the impossibility of dismissing his mutinous actions. Rumors circulated that Wilson wanted Tarp to be hanged. Anger and animosity had simmered for some time between Captain Wilson and Tarp, who enjoyed making fun of the "gimpy" old captain behind his back as a crew joke.

Judge Wilson set Tarp's trial two days after the insurrection, apparently hoping to keep the crime fresh in the minds of witnesses, and that a harsher sentence would be acceptable. Immigrants and crew members alike crowded the deck of the Thistle.

Captain Wilson limped into court overlooking his watery domain.

Following a brief overview of the uprising, Judge Wilson asked Tarp for his defense for the insurrection— perhaps astutely anticipating that Tarp had no defense. Unexpectedly, Tarp stood facing the witnesses, instead of Wilson, and declared that that his actions were defensible under the circumstances and that he had no remorse.

Tarp raised his voice to opine whether the *Thistle* had been approached by a pirate ship or, quite possibly, a ship of unfortunate souls suffering from starvation and illness. Silence fell over the crowd of downward faces, stunned by the thought that helpless individuals may have been abandoned at sea.

Realizing that he had made legal inroads with the witnesses, Tarp further raised the possibility that a "Ghost" ship had approached the *Thistle*— most likely with only a few starving survivors.

Sensing that public opinion was moving in his favor, Tarp suddenly turned as an unschooled lawyer towards Wilson and leveled a damming accusation. Tarp eloquently argued that piracy was virtually nonexistent by 1738, intimating that Wilson was surely aware of seafaring news that only in some remote regions such as Newfoundland and in years past in the Bahamas that privateering existed. No one saw a double cannon deck. No one saw a pirate flag, claimed Tarp.

Tarp continued throwing legal daggers towards his captain, and asserted that Wilson was

145

nothing more than an aging shipmaster, who may have encountered a few pirates in bygone days, but now his decision on August 9 was a "cut-and-run" act that besmirched any captain's character, and displayed lack of confidence in his crew.

The troubling redirection of guilt was enough for Wilson to cut short the proceedings, and move to a judgement. Wilson decreed to divide the witnesses into two groups—one group that favored punishment, and a second group that did not approve Tarp's actions but denounced punishment.

The mutineers were freed, but Tarp was demoted to the status of ship laborer.

Johann and Anna postponed their wedding until their arrival in Philadelphi

The Solar Eclipse

On August 15, a solar eclipse occurred over *Thistle's* waters. Observers on deck were suddenly blinded and freaked out.

The morning had begun like many others. Early risers strolled about the deck. Captain Wilson had not left his cabin. A few sailors sang worldly songs while repairing ropes. On the leeward side of the ship's stern, a religious group of twenty or thirty who had bonded during the voyage circled for their morning ritual— a service that usually began with consuming a pinch of bread, followed by an indiscriminate period of loud prayers from kneeling positions.

Their prayers were almost underway when a dark shadow moved slowly across the ocean, pulling a blanket over the *Thistle*. Everyone looked for light from the heavens and discovered that the once-large moon at Gif Teed's funeral wake was moving in front of the sun.

The gradual occlusion captivated and simultaneously hypnotized sun-seekers on deck. All were blinded by the alluring darkness. Within seconds the deck was transformed into a dance floor of blind and staggering dancers reaching for partners.

Someone loudly quoted the minister's prophecy on the Rhine River boat.

I will darken the earth in the clear day.

(Amos 8:9)

Let their eyes be darkened, that they see not.

(Psalms 69:23)

One of the prayer warriors frantically screamed that she sensed the minister was nearby. Others began to scream. Overpowered by religious fervor, the clan knelt to the deck with loud prayers, each repenting of past wrongs. The chatter of admissions seemed to cover numerous past misdeeds: vineyard fruits had been stolen, a neighbor's goat had been stolen and eaten, brow-raising infidelities

149

were admitted, scandalous lies had been told, and numerous unselfish acts were acknowledged.

Prayers ceased when fresh light beamed down, signaling divine approval. Loud cheering followed, as past deeds appeared forgiven. A spirit of goodwill pervaded the embraces, with many acknowledging that they had "found the light."

The afflicted found their way below deck, where the darkness provided some respite, although many complained of blind spots for days. The solar blindness of those on deck was so mysterious that those who had remained below deck were confused by attempted explanations. Also, Captain Wilson, who had emerged from his quarters only after the solar eclipse, looked bewildered at the blinded ones.

The impact of the solar eclipse, which occurred on August 15, carried over to August 16 when a flagless vessel dangerously approached the *Thistle*. After making an abrupt correction in course, the *Thistle* came alongside the craft, only to discover no one at the helm. Numerous young men of color were seen huddled in a state of blindness and near-nakedness. A nearby white man was seen waving and calling for help.

The encounter revealed a business of transporting young male slaves and indentured servants away from southern plantations to freedom in either Maryland or New England. The white man, who appeared to be in his fifties, revealed that his brother, a northern industrialist, made trips to rendezvous sites as far away as the Caribbean, from where young fugitives either stole or built boats to reach the freedom vessel.

Passengers on the *Thistle* learned of occasional attempts by slaves to escape from southern plantations as far away as the Caribbean. The Hope brothers financed many of the southern plantations. The following excerpt from page 62 of "The Slave History of Historical Predecessors of ABN-AMRO" (the successor bank in Amsterdam of the Hope Brothers) describes the escape of slaves.

Beginning of Excerpt: Fleeing from the Plantations

Fleeing from the plantations was more common than large-scale revolt. Sometimes, the enslaved fled for a brief period, but they also regularly tried to regain their freedom by escaping (marronage). Enslaved people even managed to free themselves in this way from plantations that were connected to Hope & Co. On islands such as St. Eustatius and St. Croix, escaping from plantations was particularly risky. These were relatively small islands with very limited opportunities for enslaved people to hide. (Note: St. Eustatius is a small Dutch island near St. Maarten). The St. Croix slave law left no doubt as to what could happen to "wicked and unfaithful slaves" who to charge of an escape attempt: first, in three different places of the island,

153

they were set upon with glowing pliers, and then they were hanged. Marronage nevertheless occurred regularly. On the Caribbean islands, the best chance enslaved people had of a successful escape was by making or stealing a boat and escaping by sea. The Spanish- island of Puerto Rico, an island with hardly any plantations in the eighteenth century, offered an opportunity for escape. The Spanish authorities were prepared to grant free status to enslaved people who converted to Roman Catholicism. To reach the island from St. Croix, however, required a dangerous boat trip of at least 100 kilometres (about 65 miles), from St. Eustatius it was 300 kilometres. That did not stop many from trying to escape slavery by this route. As Stadtholder William IV's representative of the WIC, Thomas Hope personally took political action to try to close off this escape route by putting diplomatic pressure on Spain. The Spanish government took little action, so the escape route to Puerto Rico remained open for a long time.

The fact that, on St. Croix, enslaved people escaped with great regularity is demonstrated by the frequent occurrence of "runaway-ads" in the English-language Royal Danish American Gazette. This newspaper, published on St. Croix, regularly featured advertisements about runaway enslaved people from plantations with a connection to Hope & Co. The 8 January 1777 edition, for example, contained an advertisement about nine runaways from the Jerusalem sugar plantation. The owner was also missing a canoe, and therefore assumed that the nine men had fled by sea.

Among those who fled were Johannes the sugar cook, Hercules the distiller, and Gosong the copper, mentioned earlier with respect to their stated high values in the accounts, due to their specialist knowledge. For tax purposes, owners on St. Croix had to make an annual declaration of all enslaved people on their plantation. The names of the nine escaped slave people he placed an "R" (for 'runaway'). The list for the year 1778 gives us a clue what happened to them: all the enslaved people were back to work. None of them had been executed, possibly because the planter had pardoned them due to their indispensable work on the plantation.

The document reveals somethings unusual, however: mortality on the plantation was very high in 1778. Seventeen people had died, more than ten per cent of all enslaved people, much more than in earlier years. Four of them died on 6 March, nine others in the following month. One was Quakoe, who had been among the group of escapees. The plantation must have been agitated and it is possible that the deaths were the result of a rebellion.

In the summer of 1778, three more enslaved people ran away. The unrest was still ongoing. In February 1779, a group of five people escaped— including some who had tried to escape before: "Puerto Rico" according to the planter. All these people were officially collateral for a loan managed by Hope & Co. This was clearly of no concern to them.

End of Excerpt

Thistle passengers learned that cities in the north were eager to hire low-wage labor, and that it was a blessing for the older slave families to think of a future for their boys, free of the plantations. A "divine calling" to assist young slaves in finding a new life had led the husband-and-wife team on earlier liberation journeys.

Unfortunately, two workers and the owner-investor were swept overboard a few days earlier by unusual giant waves, leaving the stranded craft without navigation. After their losses, a distraught widow and her defenseless brother-in-law found themselves adrift, with no one to guide their ship.

The blindness of the fugitive slaves appeared severe, possibly due to their confinement to an upper deck with only a small canopy. The vessel lacked remediation below deck from the eclipse, because the small hull was brimming with melons and various other fruits for sustenance.

Captain Wilson faced divided opinions regarding proper humane treatment of those in blindness aboard the sleek vessel, identified by someone as a fast-moving Bermuda Sloop. The prayer warriors favored bringing the slaves aboard the *Thistle* for a few days for hopeful remediation, citing the benefit of their own blindness. Captain Wilson yielded to the religious pressure, but many immigrants hopelessly complained the *Thistle* could not accommodate the additional number.

On the second night of the "sleepover," one of the young slaves attracted much attention with uncontrollable coughing. Shortly after daylight, he died, causing fear of possible contagion, and prompting several passengers to recall the threatening prophecy from the minister on the Rhine River boat. However, some passengers, weary of hearing about the Rhine River prophet, sarcastically asserted that the germ-laden hull of the *Thistle* could have caused the death.

Two hours later, before lowering the young slave into the ocean, the widow of the deceased industrialist prayed and sang.

After the committal service, Captain Wilson called officers on deck, where he announced the immediate departure of the fugitive vessel and its occupants. Wilson elaborated that the *Thistle* could not harbor criminal fugitives, and therefore these people would be immediately discharged. Their vessel would have former First Mate Tarp as captain, assisted by those men who had participated in the earlier mutiny. Tarp, the widow of the deceased industrialist, and her brother-in-law had privately approved the plan. Tarp showed delight with his leadership promotion and the possibility of a substantial financial reward, and his opportunity to leave the *Thistle*.

Some passengers expressed mixed emotions after overhearing the widow's comment to her brother-in-law, "We will never make money from these poor devils if they remain blind."

The city of Philadelphia, in the province of Pennsylvania, taken from the Jersey shore, 1700-1800. Artist George Heap (1715-1760). Publisher Carington Bowles (1724-1793). New York Public Library Digital Collections. The Miriam and Ira D. Division of Art, Prints and Photographs. Image ID 53923. Public Domain

The Year of Destroying Angels

September's fall colors were blazing along the Delaware as the *Thistle* glided near Washington Street Harbor, amid scenes of bobbling boats and large ships. Passengers celebrated their arrival with loud applause and indiscriminate hugs.

The *Thistle* berthed near three immigration ships, where none showed many departing passengers. Long delays before debarkation portended troubling health inspections and the likelihood of onboard sickness.

Weeks and months would pass before immigrant passengers would learn of the sickness and deaths on other ships that crossed the Atlantic during 1738.

News spread from local and northern newspapers, municipal authorities, and waiting homeland friends. Some of the more notable tragedies are described below.

- The *Gazette* reported the ship *Davy* arrived October 25 with news that the captain, two mates, and 160 passengers had died at sea. The ship's carpenter, William Patton, brought the stricken vessel up the Delaware River. Patton listed 74 men, 47 women, and no children as survivors.

- The *Andrew* under Captain John Stedman finally arrived October 29, but health inspectors deemed it unsafe to immediately release the fevered passengers to the public due to the approximately 120 deaths that occurred before the ship reached port.

- In November, a typhoid-like epidemic struck three-quarters of the passengers aboard the *Charming Nancy*.

- The *Oliver* lost 50 of its 300 passengers at sea during the crossing; most were children. A mutiny occurred nearing land where several deserters left the ship in search of food and water. While the mutineers were on land the Oliver wrecked in a sandbar where 50 drowned and 120 either drowned or froze in the January waters of 1739.

- The *Princess Augusta* wrecked off Rhode Island's Block Island on December 27, 1738. Fierce gale winds blew the 300-ton ship into a northerly course. The wreckage was never found, and the site later became a state shrine. In John Greenleaf Whitter's famous poem, the ship is named "Palatine." According to Wikipedia's account, the Augusta left Rotterdam for Philadelphia in the late season of August, 1738. Contaminated water caused a fever that killed 240 immigrants.

The above list of tragedies does not minimize the deaths and sufferings on other vessels that crossed the Atlantic in 1738.

Most historical accounts revealed that Rhine River boatsmen brought more than 6,000 Palatines to Rotterdam, but deaths at sea and before disembarking took approximately 2000 lives. An accurate accounting is difficult because children under the age of fifteen were not counted on some ships, and because some immigrants stayed in Rotterdam, while some feeble Palatines returned to their homeland following the trip down the Rhine.

Many writers, especially those documenting their German ancestors, have referred to the disastrous 1738 sailing season as "The Year of Destroying Angels," taking a verse from the Bible.

He cast upon then the fierceness of his anger, wrath, and indignation, and trouble, by sending evil angels among them. (Psalms 78:49, KJV)

The expression is believed by many to have originated from some early German writers, cited in

Klaus' classic work, suggesting that some passengers in 1738 were greedy and undeserving of life in America, while others were more faithful and deserving of a better life and justified in leaving their homeland. This author asserts that many of the immigrant deaths in 1738 occurred among the very young and the frail—hardly a target of God's wrath toward people consumed with greed.

This author views the expression "The Year of Destroying Angels" as dramatization, and presents evidence suggesting that so-called destroying angels resided and conducted business in Rotterdam, displaying their greed for wealth and support for slavery.

"GET THEM (IMMIGRANTS) OUT OF THE WAY" REFLECTED THE ATTITUDE OF CERTAIN OFFICALS IN ROTTERDAM

These were the words spoken by Jewish interests in Rotterdam. A 450% increase in the city-paid passenger fare, from 11 dinars per passenger in off years to 60 dinars in 1738, facilitated the hurried removal of immigrants (footnote 7, The Hope & Co. Wikipedia)

The flood of immigrants into Rotterdam was generally unwelcome news to city officials from the very beginning. They were initially housed in the ruins of St. Elbert's Chapel, which was located about two miles outside of the city. In addition to supposedly paid fares by the city of Rotterdam, the "redemptioner" system was implemented as an economic incentive to further expedite the exodus of poor immigrants to Philadelphia, generally on ships

owned by the Hope and Company.

THE EMPHASIS OF ROTTERDAM "TO GET THEM OUT OF THE WAY" LED TO OVERLOADING OF IMMIGRATION SHIPS

The 450% increase in city-paid passenger

fares in 1738 provided strong incentive to expedite

the removal of immigrants, with the consequent

overloading of immigrant ships. These ships became

rife with various health conditions, including typhus,

typhoid, scurvy, dehydration, and general

malnutrition.

Adding to the health problems, some ships

with large passenger loads experienced diseases and

deaths due to lack of food or water while crossing the

Atlantic. The depletion of supplies from unexpected

delays at ports or at sea exacerbated sufferings of passengers on overloaded ships.

The crowding of 200-300 immigrants inside the damp hull of ships for 2-3 months provided an environment for disease propagation. The business objective of many Atlantic voyages was to transport valuable commodities, though frequently infested with rats, " back" from the Americas to Europe. To that purpose, shippers sought an economic trade balance by increasing passenger loads(ballast) to facilitate a faster return of valued commodities to Europe.

LOGISTIC SHIPPING FAILURES LED TO SICKNESS AND MORTALITY OF IMMIGRANTS

The flood of thousands of immigrants into Rotterdam in 1738 not only created an immediate health challenge but also a logistic challenge of managing many ships.

Strassburger and Hinke's list of German immigrant ships arriving in Pennsylvania showed that 2 to 7 ships per year had crossed the Atlantic during the previous ten years, but in 1738 there were 16 crossings. A serious logistic failure was the near simultaneous arrival of overloaded immigration ships at the port of Philadelphia. A portion of the data for port arrivals demonstrates the logistic problem.

173

ARRIVAL	SHIP	PASSENGERS
Sept 16	Queen Elizbeth	300
Sept 19	Thistle	300
Sept 20	Friendship	187
Sept 20	Nancy	150

These data show that approximately 1000 passengers arrived for debarkation within a 2–3-day period. Delays in debarkation, for example on the *Andrew*, were known to cause additional suffering.

The debarkation procedure (Appendix A) appears difficult to follow for ships arriving close to one another. Following the procedure would be challenging in situations where illness was widespread, where adequate health inspectors were not available, where everyone needed to be examined, where a procession to city hall was necessary, and where language barriers were a problem. Any non-compliance could potentially disrupt the procedure.

Adding to the complexity of debarkations, some captains reported fewer emigrants onboard, to avoid a tax of 40 shillings for each emigrant that disembarked. For example, the *Gazette* reported that over 300 passengers were on the *Winter Galley*, but Captain Paynter may have reported only 252 to avoid the additional tax.

When the Grindstaffs took the Oath of Allegiance in Philadelphia the recorder listed the ancestral name of the father, Johanes Dietrich, instead of Cransdorf. Johanes Dietrich's name is listed in the signature collection in Philadelphia in the "List of German Pioneers from the twenty- five ships that disembarked between 1727 and 1775." The reason for the omission of the six Grindstaffs who made the voyage is unclear, especially since they were party to the Oath of Allegiance, but Dietrich remained in Germany. This incident indicates the debarkation procedure was not strictly followed

LOGISTIC SHIPPING FAILURES INCLUDED LAUNCHING OF SHIPS IN THE STORMY SEASON

The logistic failures in 1738 go beyond ships departing and arriving within close time intervals. During the later months of 1738, when storms were likely to occur, a few ships received permission to sail. Notably, the *Princess Augusta* wrecked off Rhode Island's Block Island on December 27, 1738. Fierce gale winds blew the 300-ton ship into a northerly course. According to Wikipedia's account, the Augusta left Rotterdam for Philadelphia in the late season of August, 1738, yet another example of "getting them out of the way."

LOGISTIC FAILURES INCLUDED THE SANCTIONING OF SHIPS NOT DESIGNED FOR SAILING THE ATLANTIC

Among the nightmarish logistic failures, some vessels, specifically bilander ships, were unfortunately sanctioned to cross the Atlantic. These two-masted ships were rarely more than 100 tons and normally sailed "bi-land" along the shorelines and canals of Holland. Only occasionally did they operate in the North Sea. The publication "List of German Pioneers" lists only 6 bilanders making the crossing in approximately 50 years. One *"bilander Thistle"* with 158 passengers successfully reached Philadelphia from Rotterdam on October 28.

However, shortly after leaving Rotterdam, the *Oliver,* a bilander weighing 120 tons and carrying 300 passengers, encountered fierce destructive winds. Upon docking at Hellevoetsluis, Captain William Walker and several passengers declined to return to the *Oliver,* citing concerns about being overloaded. Captain Wright assumed Captain Walker's position and proceeded to Chesapeake Bay, where the ship wrecked in a sandbar in January 1739, leading to the deaths of over 100 passengers in the icy waters. The Hope Brothers, owners of the *Oliver*, bribed a survivor of the wreck to speak positively about the trip, fearing a lawsuit.

The use of bilanders in 1738 may have resulted from a scarcity of ships, or desperation to leave Rotterdam, or flawed reasoning, or a combination of these.

THE OVERLOADED IMMIGRATION SHIPS BROUGHT "PALATINE FEVER" TO PHILADELPHIA

The infirmity dubbed "Palatine fever" by Philadelphians afflicted many immigrants arriving there in 1738. This fever is today referred to as typhus, which is generally transmitted by lice, fleas, and mice in unsanitary environments. In 1750, the Philadelphia Legislation restricted the number of passengers on a ship and specified the necessary space for each passenger during the voyage.

The significant arrival of immigrants afflicted with Palatine fever in 1738 prompted Provincial Governor George Thomas to advocate for the Assembly's approval of a "pest house" to efficiently quarantine the infected immigrants.

The Assembly rejected Governor Thomas'
proposal but, four years later, approved construction
of a lazaretto in 1742 to address a yellow fever
outbreak that had occurred in 1741. The 1742 "pest
house" which began as "Fisher's Island", was
renamed Province Island, and subsequently State
Island, and finally became known as the "old
lazaretto."

Numerous authorities attributed the failures
of this lazaretto to its proximity to the expanding
city, which facilitated interactions between locals and
infected individuals.

In 1799, following the devastating yellow fever
outbreak in Philadelphia in 1793, authorities
constructed a new lazaretto on ten acres in the

sparsely populated marshlands of Tinicum Township, approximately ten miles away from the first lazaretto. Byrne stated that this quarantine facility "failed miserably in curtailing the spread of yellow fever and other infectious diseases." In retrospect, since mosquitos are now known to thrive in damp areas, the choice of construction sites for the lazarettos may have been unfortunate.

There is no credible medical link between "Palatine fever" (typus) and yellow fever. The current knowledge is that Palatine fever was caused by filthy environments while the cause of yellow fever, not discovered until 1900, was by transmission from infected mosquitos. However, the "contagious" city of Philadelphia was edging closer to great peril during the late 1790s from countless numbers

coming in by ships from around the world, and the

more unsuspecting peril of mosquitos thriving in the

unsanitary marshes about the city. Ironically, the

constructed medical facilities (lazarettos) were

erected in marsh-like areas. All the while, 5000 of the

50,000 inhabitants of Philadelphia died from the

yellow fever epidemic of 1793. The central governing

body of what would become the United States

relocated to Washington DC.

It is noteworthy that in 1900 Dr. Walter Reed

discovered the relationship between mosquitos and

yellow fever. Prior to this date Dr. Benjamin Rush, a

prominent physician at the Philadelphia Lazaretto

and signer of the Declaration of Independence,

believed that yellow fever was caused by impure air. Dr. Rush's controversial proposals included aggressive bleeding, purging, and large doses of mercury.

Byrne and others provided a critical commentary on the prestige of the Philadelphia Lazaretto, presenting the following viewpoints:

1. Sailors, merchants, and newly arriving immigrants abhorred the sight of the yellow flag of the lazaretto.
2. Captains and healthy passengers hated the long waiting time for clearance to dock.
3. Long clearance times caused merchants to suffer from cargo loss.
4. Merchants became averse to a nearby lazaretto as the growing city physically approached the facility.
5. Health officials in Philadelphia became more focused on the need for sanitation aboard immigration ships.

Immigration Ships Yearly from Rotterdam

Year	No.	Year	No.	Year	No.
1727	5	1743	9	1759	0
1728	3	1744	5	1760	0
1729	2	1745	0	1761	1
1730	3	1746	2	1762	0
1731	4	1747	5	1763	4
1732	11	1748	8	1764	11
1733	7	1749	21	1765	5
1734	2	1750	14	1766	5
1735	3	1751	15	1767	7
1736	3	1752	19	1768	4
1737	7	1753	19	1769	4
1738	16	1754	17	1770	7
1739	8	1755	2	1771	9
1740	6	1756	1	1772	8
1741	9	1757	0	1773	15
1742	5	1758	0	1774	6
				1775	2

Immigrant Passenger Ships from Rotterdam in 1738 to Philadelphia, Passengers, Arrival Dates

SHIP	PASSENGERS	ARRIVAL
Catherine	15	July 27
Winter Galley	252	September 5
Glasgow	349	September 9
Two Sisters	110	September 9
Robert & Alice	320	September 11
Queen Elizabeth	300	September 16
Thistle	300	September19
Friendship	187	September 20
Nancy	150	September 20
Fox	95	October 12
Davy	121	October 25
Saint Andrew	300	October 27
Bilander Thistle	152	October 28
Elizabeth	95	October 30
Charming Nancy	100	November 9
Enterprise	120	December 6

Beyond Philadelphia

The Grindstaff families who sailed on the *Thistle* in 1738 initially settled in York, Pennsylvania, where Michael later married Catherine Van Noy.

Several internet sources list John and Anna Gohn of York County as having ten children. Konkel's publication offers more details, revealing that natives killed Anna in 1768. Barth's family settled in Lancaster County, Pennsylvania.

Michael and his grandsons lived for almost 200 years in Johnson County, Tennessee, where he died in the home of his son Nicholas Sr. President Roosevelt authorized the construction of a TVA lake/dam in 1942, which dispersed Michael's clannish descendants from their vast lands. Their lands and the nearby small town of Butler, Tennessee are under water.

SONS OF MICHAEL GRINDSTAFF (1726-1789)
AND CATHERINE

1. **Adam**

   Died in 1777 from wounds in the Revolutionary War at Brandywine Creek

2. **Jacob**

   This author's earlier work "They Came from Germany Aboard the Thistle," details his military forays into the Cherokee Nation.

3. **Michael Jr.**

   Served as corporal in the Battle of Eutaw Springs, South Carolina where Cornwallis was permanently driven from the South

4. **Nicholas Sr.**

   Served in both the Revolutionary War and the War of 1812.

Nicholas Sr. (abt. 1766–abt. 1858)—father of Nicholas Issac, Jr.

Johnson County, Tennessee, was the lifelong home of Nicholas Sr., where he acquired large land grants for his service in the Revolutionary War. His sons held these lands for nearly 200 years, until 1948. The families became wealthy from farming, harvesting timber, and mining iron ore. Nicholas Sr. fathered six children, one of whom was Isaac Junior.

Nicholas Issac, Jr. (1815-1863), father of General Grant Wilburn Grindstaff

Isaac Jr. and his neighbors lived in constant danger because of their strong union sentiments. The Confederate leadership in Nashville rejected East Tennessee's desire for secession because of the

194

critical iron supply from East Tennessee and the vital presence of local railroads. Because of the pro-Union sentiments in East Tennessee, President Lincoln approved bridge burning, which was a hanging offense. Locally, Vice President Andrew Johnson's son-in-law, Daniel Stover, led some of the efforts. Public hangings occurred. Bridges were rebuilt.

From 1861 to 1863, Confederate troops were stationed in Johnson County to control sentiments and quell guerilla fighting. Nashville leadership sent letters to Confederate President Jefferson Davis, requesting the stationing of troops in Johnson County (Appendix B). Random killings by Confederate militia bullies were quite common.

Isaac Jr. and Martha had seven children, one of whom was the locally respected General Grant Wilburn Grindstaff.

General Grant Wilburn Grindstaff (1845–1924), father of Dudley Grindstaff

Wilburn's fortunes on the ancestral lands increased near the turn of the century with the arrival of the railway station near the family home. Vast amounts of timber were shipped to northern states. However, the railway business later declined with increased availability of automobiles and more economical mining of iron ore in the North.

Wilburn and Nancy had eleven children, one of whom was Dudley.

Dudley Grindstaff (1886-1973), and son, Curtis Grindstaff (1916-1972)

In 1924, Dudley and Sarah moved into the ancestral Grindstaff home, along with their son Curtis and wife Iva. Wilburn's wife had died in 1914, and he was near blindness.

Dudley was a local magistrate for over thirty years. Curtis, a building contractor, built fine homes and upgraded the old homeplace.

In August 1941, a tropical hurricane caused catastrophic flooding of the Watauga River, which flowed through lands owned by the Grindstaffs. This flood ripped through downstream train trestles and bridges, washed away homes and barns, caused power failures, closed businesses, and destroyed livestock. Some lives were lost. The force of the river mangled the railway track, never to be replaced.

On December 17, 1941, President Roosevelt approved the construction of Watauga Dam, which was completed in 1948 following delays during the war.

The vast Watauga Lake now covers lands on which the Grindstaff families once lived, and the once charming nearby town known as "Butler."

Forced to relocate due to the construction of the TVA dam in 1948, the storyteller, Dudley, became the new neighbor of this author, who was then a teenager, and brought with him a granddaughter, now this author's wife of sixty years.

ABOUT THE AUTHOR

Earlier books authored by Reverand Hawk are "Heavenly Morning Glories" and "They Came from Germany Aboard the Thistle." He served as pastor of six churches over the last 40 years. James and Darlene (Grindstaff) Hawk have three sons and five grandchildren from their marriage of sixty-one years. Darlene's German ancestry has been inspiration for two of his books. James' formal education included graduate studies at the University of Tennessee, Knoxville, and studies at Graham Bible College. Additionally, he taught math for two years at Northeast State Community College in East Tennessee.

REFERENCES

Byrne, J. (Ed.). (2010). *The Philadelphia Lazaretto: A Most Unloved Institution*. Pennsylvania Center.

Cloyd, J. (Ed.). (2024). *The top four therapeutic uses of licorice*. Rupa Health.

Cobb, S. (n.d.). *The story of the Palatines* (Vol. 1897) [Putnam's Sons].

Culver, H. (n.d.). *The Book of Old Ships* (Vol. 1992). (Original work published 1992)

De Kok and Brandon, G. A. P. (2022). *The Slavery History of Historical predecessors of ABN AMRO Bank. An investigation into Hope & Co. and R. Mees & Zooen* Research conducted for ABN AMRO Bank by the International Institute of Social History

Diffenderffer, F. (1898). *The German Immigration into Pennsylvania through the Port of Philadelphia, 1700-1775, Part II* (Vol. 1900). EM Printing Company.

Grubb, F. (Ed.). (1987). *The market structure of shipping German immigrants to colonial America*. University of Delaware.

Hawk, J. (2016). *They came from Germany, aboard the Thistle* (2nd ed.). Lulu Publishers.

History of yellow fever [Online forum post]. (n.d.). https://asrm.org/articles/2021/may

Klaus, K. (1998). *Beyond Germanna* (Vol. 10).

Klotche, E. (1929). *Exposition of the distinctive characteristics of the Catholics, Lutheran and Reformed churches, and well as modern denominations and sects,* .Published by the Lutheran Literary Board, Burlington, Iowa

Klus, W. (1998). *The Year of the Destroying Angels: from Beyond Germanna* (Vols. 10, Number 1).

Knittle, W. (1937). *Early Eighteenth-Century palatine emigration.*

Konkel. (1997). *Internet publication, page 145 [Online forum post].*Genealogical information on Anna Rosina Gohn

Kuhn, O. (1971). *The German and Swiss settlements of colonial Pennsylvania study of the so-called Pennsylvania Dutch.* Gryphon Books.

Looijesteijn, Nijman and Tuik, H., BN and DT. (n.d.). *The slavery history of historical predecessors of ABN AMRO Bank*.

Parsons, W. (1984). *The Great Migration 1717-1754:The Ocean Crossing and Arrival in Philadelphia—Persistent Germans, a Persistent Minority.* Chestnut Books, Collegeville, PA.

Strassburger and Hinke. (n.d.). *Passenger lists 1727-1775. The contagious city.* (2012). Cornell University.

The Emigration Season of 1738—Year of Destroying Angels (Journal of German American History, Vol. 40). (1986). Society of the History of Germans in Maryland.

The Hope & Co., "Footnote 7." (n.d.).

The Ship Oliver-the true story of the 1738 voyage [Online forum post]. (n.d.). Rootsweb/~Theshipoliver.

William Penn. (n.d.). In *Wikipedia*.

APPENDIX A

The debarkation procedure for ships arriving at the Port of Philadelphia in 1738 was as follows.

1. Passengers are examined by a physician to determine whether any contagious diseases are present.

2. The new arrivals are led in procession to City Hall to render the oath of allegiance to the King of Great Britain, then returned to their ship.

3. Announcements are printed in newspapers stating how many arrivals are to be sold. Those not indentured are free of obligation.

4. Bidders make their choice among the arrivals and bargain for years of labor.

5. Those indentured are obligated to the paying merchant, who is provided with legal documentation of the transaction, which makes the indentured person the property of the merchant for the bargained period.

APPENDIX B

Copy of Letter to Confederate President Jefferson Davis from Governor of Tennessee requesting soldiers to control insurrection in Johnson County, Tennessee (home county of Grindstaff families)

NASHVILLE, November 12,1861.

His Excellency JEFFERSON DAVIS

The burning of railroad bridges in East Tennessee shows a deep-seated spirit of rebellion in that section. Union men are organizing. This rebellion must be crushed out instantly, the leaders arrested, and summarily punished. I shall send immediately about 10,000 men to that section; cannot arm larger force at present.

If you can possibly send from Western Virginia a number of Tennessee regiments to East Tennessee we can at once repair the bridges and crush out the rebellion. I hope to be able very soon to collect a large number of sporting guns in the state to arm our volunteers and will co-operate with the Government to the fullest extent of my ability in all respects. If a part only of the Tennessee troops in Western Virginia shall be sent I would prefer Anderson's brigade.

ISHAM G. HARRIS

**He was the state's first governor from West Tennessee, considered by his contemporaries the person most responsible for leading Tennessee out of the Union and aligning it with the Confederacy during the Civil War. SOURCE: The War of Rebellion: A Compilation of the Official Record of the Union and Confederate Armies. Washington Government Printing Office.

Speculations by the reader on "hidden issues" of characters and events. Some examples below

1. Why did Gif Teed not play beautiful music in the laundry at Rotterdam?

2. Who was Gif Teed?

3. What issues existed between Gif Teed and the workers at the laundry at Rotterdam?

4. What could be the explanation for the laundry owner whipping Gif Teed, followed by embracing him?

5. How did Gif Teed get into the laundry chest and taken aboard the *Thistle*?

6. Where did Gif Teed get his stylish clothing and silver necklace?

7. What were the several sources of Gif Teed's money?

8. The relationship issues between Gif Teed and Tug?

9. The issues between Captain Wilson and Tarp?

10. The issues between Tarp and the clairvoyant, and his "disappearance".

11. The issue between the clairvoyant, the passengers aboard the *Thistle,* before and after the storms at sea?

12. The issues between Forney and Pos?

13. The issue between King Louis IV and his courtiers

14. The issues among the "prayer warriors" before and after the solar eclipse?

15. The issues between Frog and Nit?

16. The confusion between "typus" and "yellow fever."

17. The issue between the first lazarettos (near downtown Philadelphia) and the new later one constructed seven miles away for the treatment of yellow fever?

18. The "bi-racial" implication of Gif Teed?